Teach Me How To Die

I grew up in North Park, so
I wanted to donate copies ~~for~~
of my first novel to the neighborhood.

Teach Me How To Die

JOSEPH RAUCH

ISBN: 0692863338
ISBN 13: 9780692863336
Library of Congress Control Number: 2017904257
Joseph Rauch Books and Stories, New York, NY

Acknowledgements

I would like to thank the following people:

Margarita Zulueta, the love of my life, for being amazing, supporting me and making the visual materials for this book

My parents, Jim and Doris, and my younger brother, Gabriel, for loving and supporting me, and helping me edit this book

Patrick Morley and Nicole Bokat, for helping me edit this book and turn it into something I could be proud of

LaVon Wageman and Susan Shapiro, for introducing me to Patrick and Nicole

Peter Schmitt, for taking a look at my manuscript, supporting my career since its beginning and being a great friend

Alice Fischetti, for taking a look at my manuscript during its early stages and providing helpful insights about the world of publishing

Monique Sterling, for helping with the cover design

Chelsea Carter and Jennie, for helping me become a decent writer

Warren Adler, for allowing me to work with him and showing me what it meant to be a successful author

Said Sayrafiezadeh, for teaching, guiding, inspiring me and helping me improve my book

*For anyone who has lost their love or resisted the
urge to do something unforgiveable*

Part 1

Walter Klein did not have a history of committing heinous acts nor did he think he would have the nerve to commit them. Yet he was sitting on his couch with blood on his clothing, bits of semen and women's hair on his pants, and a soft smile on his face. He felt unexpected relief and could not decide whether he was under some spell or that perhaps this was the kind of person he wanted to be that day. His own stench was hard to bear, but he was too tired to change clothes. He decided to climb into bed as he was.

One

Walter woke and made his routine breakfast. Light came in through the window and glinted off his knife as he cut his favorite cranberry bagel in two and placed the halves in the toaster. He wondered what would happen if he shoved the knife into the active toaster but decided it wasn't worth finding out. He imagined the blade exploring the guts of the toaster, throwing sparks around the kitchen. Some of the sparks might dance onto his shirt, igniting it rapidly. He visualized the flames burning his skin and changing its color as he struggled to remove his clothing or roll on the floor. The cranberries on the bagel evoked the color of the burnt flesh resulting from the fire. But all he could do was imagine. He had long suppressed the nerve to act.

He used the bathroom to relieve himself while he was waiting for the bagels to toast. There was a lot of blood in his urine, much more than usual. The feeling of loss made him woozy. His doctor had predicted this increase of blood loss.

"More symptoms are going to pop up if you keep refusing treatment. I know I can't force you, but please. Please think about it. I don't understand why you're doing this."

Walter felt happy seeing the red overtake the greenish yellow in the toilet rather than mixing with it. He wondered if today the cancer would finally take him. The thought of having his life taken away had been exciting for a while. It consumed him to the point where everyday objects adopted new primary purposes. A car was not for transportation. It was a weapon that could smear a man across a freeway and kill him in an instant. Construction sites were death traps. Elevators were the method of offering the height necessary for a fall to be fatal. Cancer was a relatively slow and painful death, lackluster compared to the other possibilities but seemingly guaranteed at the rate it had been ravaging him lately. It would take his life all the same, so Walter was happy to accept it as a method of delivery to oblivion.

Walter had considered suicide but ultimately decided against it. Or rather, he lacked the nerve to do it. The notion of his friends and family (mostly his mother) reacting to such a death only created more hesitations. Suicide offered a degree of control over one's death but required overcoming an immense sense of guilt. Taking his life meant ignoring the prospect of the grief and anger friends and family would experience in the aftermath. His mother concerned him most because there was a likelihood she would blame herself for his death due to their falling out a number of years ago.

He could imagine the grief when his friends and family heard the news.

"How could he do this to us? Why didn't he tell us about what he was going through? Why didn't he ask for help? Is this my fault?"

Questions like this would inevitably arise after someone disseminated the news that he had killed himself. It would pain them unnecessarily. Walter worried suicide would be a selfish option for any sane person with friends and family. He understood people who took their own lives as a result of depression and such were not necessarily being selfish. Their illness robbed them of the ability to think rationally. Walter reasoned he was not mentally ill nor had he completely lost his rationality based on the fact that he was still able to consider the effect his death would have. Suicide, in his case, would be at least somewhat inconsiderate.

Suicide also bequeathed the memory of a man who was too miserable and weak to continue on with life or one who truly believed he had no reason to continue being alive. Although Walter acknowledged the latter was true, he didn't want his friends and family to perceive him this way. He preferred having his life passively taken from him. They wouldn't have to know he had refused treatment for cancer. In fact, he had made his doctor swear not to inform his friends and family of his refusal to be treated. The doctor would only tell them he "lost the battle," which would not be a lie thanks to the beauty and practicality of semantics. A surrender is still a form of losing.

"People die. It's tragic but also a part of life, especially if it happens from disease or old age rather than murder or an accident."

Walter wanted people to adopt this line of reasoning because it would surely lessen their grief compared to suicide. They didn't know about the cancer and might be shocked to find out about it. He did not love his friends and family enough to fight for a continued life spent with them. Nonetheless, he was a considerate person and saw death as an opportunity to solidify this at least.

Walter had thoroughly validated his desire for death. This was because mentally stable people usually had two reasons for welcoming death. The first was pain. Death was the ultimate Novocain, ensuring one could not continue suffering. Terminally ill patients with indescribably painful and crippling symptoms often wished for death.

The second reason rational humans invited death was because they believed their story had ended, that it had peaked in quality. To continue living would be like adding seasons to a TV series that had concluded its main story arc. The quality was almost guaranteed to plummet. It was better to conclude the journey on a plateau before the inevitable fall. For Walter, it was a strange combination of the first and second reasons.

The smell of burnt cranberries and the sound of the toaster tray popping up summoned him to the kitchen. The toaster was broken, but he didn't feel like replacing it. He scraped the burnt pieces into the garbage and lathered on cream cheese. He could hear his wife's voice saying, *"Maybe it's not bagel season."* This is what she would have said.

Walter pulled up yesterday's Friday Tribune next to his bagel and orange juice. An older copy was next to it. "**CAN CONGRESS AVOID FISCAL CLIFF?**"

Walter liked the idea of a cliff, the exhilarating jump and acceleration of gravity that yielded a momentary feeling of flight. The only problem was the splat at the bottom and the mixture of courage, hedonism and foolishness needed to make the jump. Walter smiled at the headline before setting the paper down and heading out the door.

The abusive couple on the first floor was arguing, as was their nature, and their bird was echoing the insults. Walter could hear bits of the tiff as he strode by.

"Did you call me a 'fuck'?" hollered the husband.

"Yeah I called you a fuck, you fuck," retorted the wife.

Walter knew fuck wasn't usually a noun, but he figured the wife didn't want to back down. Instead she invented a new use for it. She must have misspoken as her mouth contorted with rage, but admitting the mistake would give the husband another opening to attack.

"You're a needle dick prick, you asshole," continued the wife, hoping her verbal assault would do permanent damage for the first time.

"Meh Needle dick," chirped the bird, which was known for repeating key phrases heard around the household.

"Shut the fuck up!"

"Don't you yell! Don't you fucking yell at the bird!" she screamed, her voice exceeding a yell.

"Don't you yell at me! You're fucking nothing!"

"Me? Look who's talking, you dropout, you worthless junkie!" Now the insults were getting more personal.

"You're worthless! I make the money around here, bitch! Without me, you'd be out on the street sucking dick for change!"

"Oh yeah. You're soooo successful." The sarcasm blatted her words like an instrument missing a note.

Walter rolled his eyes at the dysfunction as he approached his car and escaped. Both the husband and wife had curly black hair touched with blotches of grey. The grey became more dominant each time he saw them. Walter wondered how the couple could coexist without experiencing daily aneurysms. Stress migrated the healthy pink tones of their skin to their eyes, leaving them a ghoulish color.

He rarely saw the couple, though. The husband was pleasant in person, which made Walter despise him more. Walter assumed he bottled up his rage and saved it for his wife while putting on a façade of kindness for everyone else. The wife was hideous and hostile toward everyone. She once pushed Walter out of her way and hissed, "Watch where you're going, asshole," on her way back to the building. He despised her less because she was consistent.

Walter hopped into his red Prius. His friends and co-workers at the warehouse he managed had labeled it a "pussy car," but Walter didn't care. It was comfortable, saved money on gas and rarely had any problems. Most importantly, he and his wife had decided on it together. He thought it would be best to get a grey one because grey was unassuming and less likely to have jackers contemplate theft. His wife insisted on red, though. He was glad because red was his favorite color.

"So let the cops pull me over. I'm hot, so I'll get out of my tickets. You'll have to be more careful, though. Besides, I thought you liked red. I picked it for you, babe."

He enjoyed this quality in his wife. She pushed him to be more spontaneous and challenged him without making him feel like less of a man. She had once said, "I think women want guys who are nice but not boring." This meant that she loved to see occasional aggression and assertiveness from Walter so long as it wasn't directed toward her. She loved to watch him play football with his friends. He always looked over to her after he made a good tackle so he could see that look on her face that said, "I'm definitely joining you in the shower when you get home."

The radio turned to classic rock as he started the car. "The Logical Song" by *Supertramp* came on. 105.7 The Walrus, Walter's favorite radio station, had played it almost every day that week, but he was still happy to hear it. It was a great song.

Walter was headed to pick up a woman many people assumed was his girlfriend. They spent time together the way a couple would, but Leslie would not describe herself as Walter's girlfriend and had no desire to consummate the relationship. Walter's friends and co-workers had pointed out she was taking advantage of him.

"I'm telling you, man. She's a gold-digger," said his friend and fellow band member, Kyle.

"Walt isn't even rich, though. She's more like a nickel digger," said another band member.

7

Walter met Leslie after his Jazz band, "Bad Cabbage," had finished a set at Dizzy's, a club in the northern part of San Diego. Walter picked the name after Kyle farted during rehearsal and Walter said it smelled like bad cabbage. The band members thought the name was funny and strange enough to get some attention, so it stuck. They may have been grown men, but there was a spirit of immaturity and juvenile humor in many of their conversations and mannerisms. The name put a lot of people off, but the band members didn't mind because they were performing more for fun than money. Initially, it was more about being themselves than satisfying an audience. This changed gradually, though. Women became prizes for good performances because, amazingly enough, there were people out there who thought middle-aged men playing jazz was sexy.

Walter first saw Leslie when she attended one of their gigs. He knew she was was there to see Al, the leader and drummer of Walter's band. Al was also the man she was fucking, but he left without paying her bill and wasn't answering her calls. Unfortunately for Leslie, he was indifferent to her obsequious nature.

"Your card has insufficient funds," said the bartender as he handed Leslie's debit card back to her over the greasy counter. "Maybe we can try another one or cash if it's on you."

Leslie froze as she realized her paycheck must not have transferred yet, meaning that the scraps left in her checking account weren't enough to cover the bill. Her bank had refused her a credit card, so her debit card was all she had at the time.

"I...umm...maybe I have some cash on me," she stammered. She rifled through her purse even though she knew her salvation would not be there. It was only an attempt at stalling for time. The bartender pitied her and thought about hailing his manager to see whether they could work something out.

"I'll take care of it, Andre."

Walter entered the scene gently yet assertively. He held out forty dollars in cash, more than enough to pay for everything. Leslie looked up at the stranger with confusion and gratitude.

"Thank you," said Leslie.

"Don't worry about it," said Walter.

He stared awkwardly at her for a few moments before continuing.

"So, would you mind if I asked you something?"

"Sure, go ahead. Thanks again for helping me out by the way."

"Well, I don't want you to think I only helped you so you could return some favor. Umm…we should hang out though, if that's OK."

"Oh, sure. I'll give you my number."

"It's not a date or anything like that," blurted Walter. "I just want to see more of you."

Leslie gave him a puzzled expression.

"Sorry. I'm being weird," continued Walter.

"No, it's OK. I'd be happy to see you again."

And so began a strange relationship people often mistook for a romantic one. Walter took her out to dinner and chauffeured her around. He made no attempts at anything physical, didn't seem interested in talking to her, and even admitted to his friends that her personality wasn't much to speak of. Happy to have someone to help her survive on her measly receptionist wages, she accepted Walter into her life without questioning his motives. She called him when she wanted something for free. He obliged as long as it meant he could look at her. Today was no different.

He pulled up to her apartment and called her on her cell. She came down the stairs in a blue denim skirt with a black top and brown jacket.

"How's it going, Walt?"

"Fine."

Not another word passed between them until they arrived at the restaurant. Walter snuck glances at her during red lights, as if they were strangers. They had a reservation at The Mission, a restaurant in North Park critics praised for its brunch. Leslie and Walter strode past the long lines and ordered pancakes and orange juice.

"So Walt, are you busy tomorrow morning?"

"No, not really. I have practice with the guys again, but that's not 'til later. What do you need?"

"Hey, why are you assuming I need something? There could be other reasons why I'm asking." She said this playfully.

They may not have had a romantic relationship, but it was at least a friendship. Walter spoke to her enough to understand her inflections and occasional use of sarcasm.

"Come on, Leslie. What do you need?" He smiled and rolled his eyes, amused with her banter but not interested in continuing it much longer.

"All right, fine. I need you to drive me up to this club in La Jolla. Al's doing a gig there and I want to see it."

"He is? I didn't know about that."

Leslie became disturbed.

"Oh yeah. Umm…he only told me about it, I think."

"Really? If he's doing a gig then he would've told me and the guys about it. He never does solo gigs, as far as I know."

"Maybe he's trying new things."

"Hmm…maybe," replied Walter. "I guess you want an excuse to see your boyfriend." Walter decided to tease her a bit. The change in topic had rekindled his interest in conversing with her.

"He's not my boyfriend," retorted Leslie, not realizing she was blushing.

"Sure he's not," continued Walter. "You don't need to deny anything. It's not like I care."

"You wouldn't care if I was messing around with him?" said Leslie, starting to become a bit bothered by Walter's attitude.

"You *are* messing around with him and I do not care." Leslie looked down at her lap in shame and was silent for a bit before continuing.

"Sometimes I think about stopping. I know everyone thinks he's a jerk," said Leslie, finally admitting her affair. "I don't get how that doesn't bother you. Aren't we technically dating?"

"We're two people spending time together. We've been over this before," Walter replied lazily.

"But why then? Why…?

"What do you want me to say?" interrupted Walter, his voice uncharacteristically biting, almost snarling. "That I'm insane, that I'm a glutton for punishment or an idiot, that I'm just a nice guy who wants to take care of you.

It's none of your business. If it bothers you so much, go find someone else to drive you around and help you until you're less worthless."

Eavesdroppers around the restaurant looked at the strange couple as Walter's voice rose. Tears slid down Leslie's cheeks as she ruminated on his words. The widower was immediately appalled at his behavior. The darkness inside him was ebbing out a bit at a time, casting its shadow in the form of hurtful words. His wife, who once acted as the levee for the parts of himself he feared, was now gone. Walter had not succeeded in rebuilding that levee, despite his best efforts.

"Look, I have my reasons for spending time with you. I just don't want to discuss them. All I was trying to say before is that you don't need to worry about me. You can do whatever you want. I don't want anything from you except your company. That's it. I didn't mean to hurt your feelings. I'm sorry."

Walter fetched a napkin so she could dry her tears.

"It's OK," said Leslie. "I shouldn't have pressed the issue. You've told me before that you didn't want to talk about it. I appreciate you helping me out by the way. I guess, given my experiences, it's hard for me to believe a guy would do anything nice for me like this without some sort of ulterior motive. That's why I keep asking."

Walter paid the bill and studied her features as she swung her purse string over her shoulder and headed to his car. He always gazed upon her like a precious old photograph, naked with no frame or lamination to protect it, not capable of living forever in a cloud or on a computer. This photo was not to be touched, only observed. Smudging would violate the memory it represented.

Leslie turned to him and kissed his cheek as they pulled up to her apartment. After processing the unfamiliar feeling of her lips, Walter jerked his head away as if her touch were violating him. This reaction puzzled Leslie. She assumed he was still upset, so she disclosed a little more to heal their relationship.

"It might not seem like it, but I'm trying every day to change things. I want to be able to live well without depending on anyone else. I actually have an interview for this admin job on Monday. It'll pay a lot more if I get it, not enough to take care of all of my debts, but more than enough to keep my head above water."

"Good luck. Do you need a ride to it?"

"Nope. There's a bus that goes pretty close. I might ask for a ride back though if that's OK. It's close to your job."

"That's fine."

He dropped her off and headed to the local community college where his band reserved a room on Saturdays from two to four. They normally only practiced once a week. This week, however, they had reserved the room for Saturday and Sunday because they had a big gig coming up.

Walter entered the room and saw his fellow band members were in the middle of a conversation. They didn't notice him entering, so they continued.

"So it looks like we're going to be playing The Pretentious Giraffe next week," said Al. Kyle chimed in at the mention of the club.

"Geez, who comes up with these names?"

"I asked the guy the same thing. He said the owner wanted the idea to be that giraffes look down on people," replied Al, shrugging as he finished his sentence.

"Yeah 'cause people are *totally* going to get that without asking," Kyle said, sarcastically.

"I think it's part of this formula restaurants and bars often use for their names. You know, 'the' and then an adjective and then an animal. Think of all the places we remember best: The Tipsy Crow, The Fat Black Pussy Cat. The list goes on and on, you know," Al said.

"The Flaccid Flamingo," muttered Walter as he approached Kyle and Al. He was comfortable intruding on their conversation because the three of them had enjoyed many silly chats like that in the past.

"What?" replied Al.

"Nothing. Just testing the formula," said Walter. He felt bad for intruding but couldn't help but indulge a moment of humor that he knew would put a little life back into him.

Al and Walter laughed. Kyle slunk away, avoiding eye contact with Walter.

12

"Hey, Walt. I need to talk to you for a minute?" The smile from their laughter left Al's face.

"What's up, Al?" replied Walter as he settled into the piano bench and took out his *Real Book*.

"So did you get the email I sent you this morning?"

"No. I had to leave for brunch so I must've missed it."

Al scratched his left temple for a moment before he continued. "I don't know how else to tell you this…but we don't need you in the band anymore."

"What?"

"It's just that we want to do other stuff besides *Real Book* songs and standards and we noticed you keep having trouble with that. You're a great piano player, Walt. We just want someone more versatile."

Walter understood why Kyle was moping around in the corner of the room and observing Al and himself through the corner of his eyes.

"I still want all of us to be friends, Walt. I just think it's better if we have someone different on piano."

"Yeah I get it."

Walter threw his books into his bag and made for the door. He was mildly upset. Nonetheless, he also immediately processed it warmly as yet another reason why death was welcome.

"I'm sorry man," said Kyle as Walter passed the threshold and headed for the parking lot.

The room became lively again as Walter left, as if his presence had increased its gravity, pulling the light from the ceiling and pushing it through the floor. The old Walter had the opposite effect. He appeared with an unrivaled energy: remembering birthdays, offering assistance with any task, smiling and playing off jokes. Now his behavior was contrived, like he was some specter pretending to be alive.

When his band mates met his late wife, they understood the source of his energy. Susan was bursting with kindness no one could rebuke. She took pleasure in helping others or bringing joy to their lives with her love of music.

Her voice entranced the band every time she sang with them. During rehearsals, the rhythm section would lose time and the horns would forget to come in because focusing completely on their notes meant missing a moment of her melody. In every place she entered, Susan was the sun. And when a star dies, a black hole takes its place, a creature that unintentionally sucks the light from everything around it.

Walter didn't know what to do with himself when he got home. He had planned on having dinner and drinks with the guys after practice and then heading home or passing out on Kyle's couch if he was too drunk. He decided to pass the time by jogging and then catching up on the seventh season of *Dexter*. The writers had ended the sixth season with a cliffhanger where Dexter's adopted sister, Deborah (who is apparently in love with him), catches him murdering another serial killer. Walter knew this would change the dynamic of the entire show and wasn't happy to see how the seventh season was going.

The show was always fun, though. It allowed Walter to put himself in Dexter's place and have some of his murderous curiosities and fantasies play out in his living room.

Walter cried out as he felt a horrible pain in his stomach and rushed to the bathroom. A mass of bloody stool and urine erupted from him the moment he sat down. He broke out into a cold sweat as he struggled not to pass out on his bathroom floor. He managed to stand up but couldn't reach to flush the toilet. The toilet seemed further away with every second passing. He crashed into his wall and it brought the toilet back into focus. Walter began to pass out again and used the last of his strength to stumble into bed. He lost consciousness the moment he felt his face on the sheets. He had never fallen asleep so quickly.

Two

Walter found himself standing in the middle of a somewhat crowded street. He looked around for an indication of where he was but couldn't find anything. The street signs were blurry to the point of illegibility and the asphalt was pixilated. Every house on the block was identical; one story, grey roofs and white walls with a central door and a window on each side, utterly dull. The people around him moved like phantoms, almost floating instead of walking. They drifted nearly in unison, more like a river of flesh and clothing than a crowd of living beings. As he walked forward, his surroundings began to flicker rapidly, as if he were looking at an extremely fast slide slow or an old film that required a crank to operate. He assumed it was a dream. It was, however, more vivid than any dream he had experienced. Most of his dreams were flashes compared to what he was seeing now. With this experience, Walter believed he would be able to remember every detail upon waking up as if he had watched a video of the scene.

A well-dressed man emerged from the stream of phantoms. His aura was intimidating, like that of a wild beast that had been painstakingly housebroken. This man was a violator disguised as a gentleman. Id ruled him, consumed him, drove his every action. Glut, pleasure, and indulgence saturated him without swelling his figure, nor sitting on his skin. This man was the embodiment of many qualities Walter desired and feared. He was the improbable but vaguely possible result of all the impulses Walter had suppressed for more than a decade. Consequences meant nothing to him. There were only desires and the most expedient means of indulging them. Empathy was of no value to him. It was only a hindrance.

Muscles laced his body in an outline so nearly perfect it could have been machine-drawn. An expensive suit hugged them. To Walter, he appeared a complete stranger, that is, until he analyzed the man's facial features. He had Walter's unique combination of slick black hair from his father and bright green eyes and Latin features from his mother.

"Hello, Walter," said the possible doppelganger.

"Um…Hi. Do I know you?"

"I'm hurt, Walter. Don't you remember me?"

"Sorry. I wish I did."

"We worked together. Remember? I was there when we defeated that man. We made him bleed together and you accepted my help. We gave that miserable piece of shit what he deserved. We showed him that he was beneath us, that he was unworthy to breathe the same air. That was when we met. But I've known you. I've known you your entire life. You gave birth to me when you began to wonder about all those seemingly forbidden things, those tingling taboos you became so adept at swatting when they buzzed around."

"I-I remember now." The man's words were lulling Walter into a state of docility. There was something soothing about them. Walter tried to resist.

"Yes, that's good. So will you accept me again? It's been so long. We have so much to do and such a small window of opportunity. Won't you let me help you again?"

"What do you want me to do?"

"*We*, Walter; you and I. We are different parts of a whole and I want us to collect on what we have earned. I want us to murder and humiliate. I want us to visit a hell upon all the unworthy pieces of shit that contaminate our world."

Walter knew exactly what he meant. The proposition was exciting, thrilling, almost titillating. It nearly enticed him into quick acceptance until he recalled the one time he had indulged his violent urges. As he thought about the consequences of his one violent act, his desire stopped swelling. It faded as he took deep breaths and looked away from the ethereal man. For a moment, he had the strength to refuse.

"Um, I'm alright. I think I'm ready to wake up now."

"Are you denying me, Walter?" said the man as he stepped closer.

"Well, yeah I guess I am," replied Walter as he backed away and attempted to wake up.

"I suppose it was my mistake to phrase my demands as questions. Frankly, you have no choice. I am a part of you and you will accept me whether you want to or not."

Walter felt hands and arms form around him. Before he could react sufficiently, several men were holding him in place. Two of them bound his arms and the others attached themselves to his legs and waist. Another two appeared and held his upper body and head still. The other people on the street walked by Walter and could not seem to hear his shouts. He screamed until the strange figures grasped his neck, causing him to wheeze.

"Now it's my time. Now it's our time. I've spent my entire existence in anticipation of this moment. Take me. I am yours. You want it. It is time," continued the polished clone as he neared Walter with an ecstatic grin. The strange man grasped Walter's face with his left hand.

"Now, open your mouth."

The man reached his right index finger into Walter's mouth. Walter bit down with as much force as possible. The strange man cackled with pleasure and began to wriggle his finger further into Walter's teeth so the wound continued to open, causing increasing amounts of blood to drip onto the concrete and run down his arm.

"Yes! Yes, Walter! This wouldn't be any fun if you were that kind of man! This wouldn't be any fun at all if you were the kind of man who would accept me so easily! You wouldn't be Walter Klein if I could tempt you with such little effort! I would savor this moment for eternity, but I mustn't waste time. Now, give in to me. Give in to your curiosity and all those dark, delectable thoughts you entertained."

Walter felt another hand grasp his nose and he was forced to relinquish his grip and gasp for air. The moment his jaw loosened, another pair of hands grabbed it and forced it to remain open. The strange man slipped his arm down Walter's throat and forced his entire essence inside Walter's body as if he were made of paste. Walter was being filled up and felt he could explode into a pile of flesh at any moment.

Three

Walter opened his eyes. His cheek was wet. He rolled over to see a dark spot of drool soaked into his sheets. He checked the time and realized he must've slept for at least twelve hours because it was already afternoon. He panicked for a moment as the memory of last night tickled his insides. He removed his clothing and saw several stains of blood in his underwear. Nonetheless, he felt fine. He had a sense of urgency in starting the day. More than anything, he was hungry. His stomach seemed to be collapsing like a dying star, eating itself because it didn't have the patience to wait for food.

Walter leapt out of bed and ran to the kitchen. He consumed a bagel in five minutes and then headed to the bathroom to shower off yesterday's sweat, dirt and blood. He urinated before getting in the shower and was surprised to see clear, healthy liquid in the toilet. He was out of the shower in five minutes and decided to head to the nearby diner. Walter couldn't understand the feeling of urgency he was experiencing. It was like a current was sweeping him along. He had no desire to fight it.

The sprinklers were running in the lawn in front of Walter's apartment building. The abusive couple was standing near it, watching the rainbow created from the sun hitting the water at the right angle.

"Hi," said the wife to Walter, gruffly as usual.

"Hey," replied Walter without looking at her. He had plans for the couple, but that would have to wait. He couldn't afford to get distracted by them at the moment.

"Hi," chimed the husband in a disgustingly pleasant tone.

Walter was silent. He heard the husband but didn't feel like replying to him.

"He said 'Hi' to you," barked the husband once he thought Walter was out of earshot.

"Yeah so."

"You said 'Hi' to him and he said 'Hi' to you and then I said 'Hi,' but he didn't say 'Hi' back."

"Will you shut the fuck up and enjoy the rainbow?"

"But he didn't say 'Hi' to me."

"Enjoy the rainbow!"

"Why would he say 'Hi' to you and not to me? What's so great about you?"

"He meant it for both of us, asshole. Now enjoy the rainbow!"

"No he didn't, you bitch."

Walter caught a bit of their conversation as he clambered into his car to seek out the nearest source of filling food. He peeled out into the street as aggressively as he could or rather as much as one could possibly do in a Prius.

A Palestinian family owned the nameless diner in Walter's neighborhood. The sign merely said "DINER" and everyone in the neighborhood just called it "The Diner" because it was the only one. The owner was pleasantly surprised to see Walter because he hadn't eaten there since his wife's passing. Walter hadn't told many people about his wife's passing so the people at the restaurant were unaware.

"Walter! Long time no see, buddy. Table for two?"

"Only one this time, Najib."

"Oh, OK," said Najib, slightly confused but not willing to press the matter.

Walter took his seat. An unfamiliar waitress approached him.

"I'll have two Belgian waffles with sausage, eggs, and a muffin. Oh and some hash browns and toast."

"Is someone else arriving?"

"Nope. It's all for me. I'm starving."

Walter scanned her as she took his order and removed her eyes from him. She looked a lot like Najib and Walter correctly assumed she was his daughter.

Walter took his time with the brunch. His hunger hadn't subsided much, but he still forced himself to savor the food the way a death row inmate would during a last meal. Once he finished, he strode out of the restaurant without paying the bill and headed to his next stop.

Walter realized he was already terribly late to pick up Leslie. Still, he approached her apartment without worry and knocked on the door.

"What the fuck, Walt? You were supposed to pick me up like three hours ago. I called you five times."

"Mind if I come in?" Leslie was visibly surprised that Walter had ignored her and neglected to apologize in one sentence. She let him enter, however, in the hopes there would be a latent apology or an attempt to make it up to her. She was worried as well. It was uncharacteristic of Walter to be late and unresponsive.

"Sure," replied Leslie as she opened the door.

Walter sat on her ragged loveseat and put his feet on her small coffee table without asking permission or removing his shoes. Leslie became frightened as she watched his abnormal behavior from her kitchen counter.

"You know I had a revelation while I was driving here."

"What's that?"

"I realized why I shouldn't waste my time with a cunt like you."

"Excuse me?" Leslie looked as though she had just heard a very bad joke at a funeral.

"You're excused. And don't pretend like you didn't hear me."

Leslie's lower lip quivered as she struggled to understand what was happening. "I-I think you should leave."

Walter ignored her and continued, determined to finish his sentiment.

"You look like my wife. You look like my dead wife and that's why you're in my life. I was hoping that if you looked like her then maybe you would be like her and I could marry you and things would go back to normal. But you're not like her at all. You only look like her. You're not even a fraction of the woman she was. She was kind, considerate, funny, smart, a brilliant music professor…and you're a selfish cunt. It's like the world was playing some sick fucking joke on me by having me run into some copycat. Anyway, the point is you look like her and that's why I waste my time and money on you. I'm a sucker for nostalgia. Maybe you feel like her too."

Leslie was in a trance of disbelief as Walter approached her. She didn't react until he took a hand full of her hair with his right hand and made circles in it with his thumb, attempting to cross-reference the texture with memories of his wife. She woke from her trance and pushed his hand away. He could tell she wouldn't allow him to do as he pleased while she was conscious. He decided to remedy this obstacle.

Walter knew the first strike was key. He had to attack her in a way that would surprise her so she wouldn't think to defend herself. Walter pretended to withdraw his hand and turned his body as if he were preparing to leave. He was actually revving up to slap her with his backhand. Walter winced as he struck her and felt her tooth cut his knuckle. She was thrown off balance and went crashing into her wall. Walter continued his assault before she could recover her footing. In a matter of seconds, she was wailing on the floor, struggling to get up. Walter marveled at how easy it was and how amazing the rush of adrenaline felt. He then grabbed her toaster from the counter perpendicular to the wall and used it to club away the last of her consciousness until she was face down on the floor.

Walter turned her body over with his feet so that he wouldn't get easily noticeable amounts of blood on him. He removed her clothing without care and flung the articles across the room. He felt every inch of her body with his hands before using his own body.

Walter was disappointed. She didn't feel like his wife. Not at all.

Walter used her bathroom to wash up before heading to his next stop. He grabbed her kitchen knife before leaving, glad to have another chance to pick one up because he forgot to grab a weapon from his own apartment. His phone indicated he had enough time to make it to the community college before his band finished their late afternoon practice. It was almost four, but Walter knew they always went over time.

Walter wasn't capable of feeling remorse or hesitation in his current state. He only felt pleasure and relief. It reminded him a bit of crying as a child, the way weeping relieved frustration, anger and sadness. In this case, each indulgence of cruelty and bloodlust acted as a tear flowing from his eyes, gradually releasing the flood he had stored behind the sockets. He would only be satisfied once all the heinous deeds, pent up curiosities, and vicious desires poured forth and completely drained the salty water. He had no idea what force was pushing him nor did he have the strength to stop it.

People were beginning to pack up their instruments when Walter arrived. Walter looked over to see the piano bench and drummer stool empty. Walter deduced that Al and Kyle either didn't get a new piano player yet or that the drummer and piano player had left. Al and Kyle noticed Walter as he ventured deeper into the room.

"Walt, what are you doing here?" began Al.

"Nothing much. I just finished giving your whore a nice cream pie and thought I'd stop by here." More of the figurative tears streamed out as Walter used the kind of vitriolic language he'd only heard in his mind before. It was exhilarating for him to hear the words aloud.

"What?"

"Never mind. I shouldn't digress. That's not why I'm here after all."

Walter picked up Al's saxophone from its stand and began fiddling with the keys. Al was about to attack Walter until Kyle stepped in.

"Walt, put that down, dude. I know you're mad, but that thing's expensive. Let's talk outside. I'll take you for a drink or something. Trashing Al's sax isn't gonna make you feel any better."

Walter planned on using the same trick as before. He pretended to set down the saxophone, prompting Kyle to approach him with relief and a lowered guard. As Kyle entered his range, Walter swung the saxophone like a club and broke Kyle's nose.

"Fuck!" yelped Kyle as he staggered back and clutched his nose.

Al rushed in and tackled Walter before he could strike again with the saxophone. They tussled on the ground. Al managed to stay on top and pin Walter's lower body to the ground. Al focused on striking his face and didn't notice Walter drawing the kitchen knife from his pocket. Walter plunged the knife deep into his gut and watched Al's face twist. Al's stopped his assault and attempted to pull the knife from his body before he collapsed. Walter twisted the knife as he saw Al's attempt. Al howled and rolled off of Walter with the knife still in him. Al's back had blocked Kyle's view until this point. Kyle opened his mouth in horror for a moment and then rushed to subdue Walter. Walter pulled the knife out of Al and brandished it before Kyle could reach him.

"Jesus fucking Christ, Walter! What's wrong with you? Al! Al! You still there? Stay with me!"

"I don't think he'll be saying anything anytime soon," said Walter as he walked toward Kyle with a grin. Al had given Walter some blows that would bruise later but Walter wasn't in any debilitating pain and was determined to finish his onslaught.

"Why are you doing this, Walt? Please, man. It's not too late."

"I just felt like it. I don't know how else to explain it. This whole day I've felt free to do what I want. And right now, I really feel like killing you. I want to see how it will happen. I want to know what kinds of sounds you'll make before you die."

Kyle reached the height of desperation and made a final plea. He was panting, more from shock than exhaustion.

"Walt, I know you're upset. I'm sorry I wasn't a man about telling you we were gonna kick you out. I felt bad about it. It wasn't my decision! I swear! You're my friend first, man! Don't do this! We can still save Al! He might not be dead!" Walter ignored Kyle's sputtering and continued advancing.

Kyle saw there was no point in persuading Walter to stop, so he attempted to run for the door. Walter cut him off by flailing the knife. This backed him into the corner with the drum set. Kyle threw the snare drum at Walter, allowing a second for him to pick up the stand and use it to defend himself. Walter, however, was determined to keep him in the corner by continuing to swing the knife.

Both men panted and stared silently at one another for several seconds before Walter felt the impetus to attack. He lunged at Kyle and caught the drum stand as Kyle parried. Walter tried to stab Kyle, but he stopped the blade by dropping the drum stand and using both hands. Walter struggled to find more reserves of power for a moment before he saw the tip of the blade enter Kyle.

Joseph Rauch

Kyle saw it enter as well. The shock loosened his grip, allowing Walter to bury it in Kyle's chest. Like Al, Kyle fell on his back in a last effort to preserve his life and keep the knife from going in further, attempting to push Walter back with his legs. Walter observed this and promptly pummeled the knife further in. He watched as Kyle's eyes became blank. Then he went to check on Al. He had been dead for minutes and had the same open, lifeless eyes.

Walter collapsed on the floor and took a moment to rest. The smell of the layers of blood caked onto his shirt became a nuisance, so he removed it. The murderous force had become less intense now, but it was still pushing him along, preventing him from feeling remorse or processing the consequence of his butchering. It would not give him rest, not yet.

Walter dashed to his car and put on the jacket he had in his passenger seat. He drove home and was about to head up the stairs and into his apartment when he heard the abusive couple arguing.

"The fuck? What the fuck am I supposed to do with this?"

"I thought you'd like it, you asshole."

"It doesn't fit, you bitch. It doesn't fucking fit! How am I supposed to wear something that doesn't fit?"

Walter knocked on the door and the husband answered.

"Hi, what can I do for you?" said the husband with a forced smile. Seeing the pretense of kindness reminded Walter of his loathing for the husband. He could feel the desire for violence bubbling.

"I want you and your ugly wife to shut the fuck up forever." He said it with a subtle hostility in his voice as if he was attempting to mug a stranger on the street without drawing attention from bystanders. The husband's eyes widened for a moment. He was shocked but quickly complied, confirming Walter's hypotheses that he could only displace his rage inside his home.

"I-I'm really sorry, sir. We'll try and keep it down."

Seeing this display of spinelessness in contrast to the cruelty he reserved for his wife catalyzed Walter's rage until it spiked. Walter kicked the door open and punched the husband in the gut, causing him to double over in pain. Walter took the opportunity to bash his head into the side of the door and then delivered a flurry of punches to ensure he stayed down.

24

Walter was surprised to the see the wife petrified, huddled into a corner. She had plenty of time to grab a knife from the kitchen or at least scramble for her phone, but she didn't.

"I'm surprised you're this scared. I thought you'd be used to seeing violence in your home."

Walter then realized this might be the first time she had witnessed physical violence in her home. He knew her husband was a verbal abuser but had never observed any bruises on the wife. Nonetheless, he couldn't be sure. He knew abusive men often took measures to hit their victims in places where others wouldn't see the bruises. The increasingly loud shrieking of the bird swatted these thoughts away. Walter decided to silence it.

"No. Please don't. Please," whimpered the wife as she saw Walter opening the cage and taking hold of the shrieking bird.

Walter took the bird by its feet with his left hand so it wouldn't be able to claw him and then attempted to break its neck with his right hand. He ignored the flapping wings and stopped trying to twist the neck after the quick realization that birds could twist their heads pretty far around. Instead, he simply tried squeezing on its neck until it ceased moving.

"Please! Please!" wheezed the wife as the bird's wings ceased fluttering.

Walter breathed a sigh of relief as he dropped the lifeless bird on the carpet and advanced toward the wife.

"I can't even tell you how good it feels to shut that noisy bird up."

The wife didn't seem to be listening to him. She was lost in her sobs.

She raised her head and muttered, "You killed her. You killed my bird. You killed Paris." Her sobs stifled further speech and she retreated her head back into her arms. Walter laughed loudly and made no effort to restrain it.

"So you're more upset about the bird, huh? Your husband, the guy you supposedly love, is over there bleeding on the floor, maybe dying, maybe even dead already, and you're pissed about some stupid, useless piece of shit bird."

Walter continued to laugh.

"Why did you marry that guy anyways? Was it money? No, what am I talking about? We live in the same building. Maybe you just like it deep down. Maybe you wanted someone to make you feel that way. Oh well. You've probably had plenty of chances to spend time with a real therapist, so I won't start now. You like being hurt, don't you? I'll oblige then."

He prepared to strike her but stopped as he processed the scene of the verbally battered woman crying in the corner. It reminded him of his mother and his hatred for her former boyfriend. The thought made him nauseous enough to halt his assault. A part of his normal self had restrained the strange man who possessed. His violent energy and morbid curiosity had almost been completely discharged. The reservoir of tears was drained.

"Shit," hissed Walter as he turned away and made for the door. Walter dragged the husband's body out of the way and exited. He knew he shouldn't be giving the wife an opportunity to call the police but he couldn't force himself to think logically.

What would happen to the bodies of the people he killed? What punishment would Walter receive? Had anyone witnessed his crimes? These questions failed to affect him. They washed over him without creating any sort of stress. Walter couldn't understand this phenomenon nor did he have the desire to question it. He was still enjoying the feeling of release and indulgence of curiosity.

Walter staggered up the stairs and entered his own apartment. A craving for sleep overwhelmed him. He collapsed on his bed as he had done the night before. He couldn't think about what he had done. He was unconscious after only a few seconds.

He had jumped off the cliff and hit the bottom. Where was the splat?

Part 2

Walter had no dreams that night. He woke up in bed completely naked. He felt clean and light. He felt purged, as if he had emptied himself without pain or discomfort, only relief.

"What's going on?" muttered Walter as he looked below the sheets to see his uncovered genitals. His clothes had completely vanished.

"You've passed on, Mr. Klein. This is the afterlife."

The voice startled Walter, causing him to become tangled in his sheets. A tall man sat in the corner of Walter's bedroom on an office chair and watched Walter as he wriggled around in his bed, threw his sheets off, and tumbled onto the floor. He wore a blue collared shirt, black pants and brown shoes. His eyes and hair matched his shoes. The hair was perfectly cut and almost seemed as if it had been cultivated. A prominent widows peak made his age ambiguous. It was unclear if the hair was receding or if it only appeared that way. His resting expression was an ugly scowl. Still, he was handsome.

Walter covered his crotch and screamed, "Who the fuck are you? What did you do to me? Where are my clothes? Damn it! I-I'll mess you up if you come any closer! I swear!"

The man in the corner was completely indifferent to his threat. His shoulders did not rise in reaction to Walter. Apathy weighed them down and masqueraded as relaxation.

"Please calm down, Mr. Klein. Your clothes are in the dresser. You may pick one outfit for your journey, so I suggest you choose wisely."

Walter became calm as the man spoke. It was as if his breath was blowing anesthetic gas across the room and suppressing all subsequent questions. Walter found himself unable to speak and compelled to follow the man's order.

"Allow me to explain the situation, Mr. Klein. First of all, I apologize for forcing you into a state of docility. I have guided many souls and learned, through experience, it is much easier to force the soul into a state of calm rather than waiting. As I said before, you are dead and what you are experiencing now is the afterlife. This is a dimension created by The Truth designed to process souls such as yourself after they leave their respective bodies. The soul processing is supposed to feel like the physical plane so the passing soul can relate to its experiences. My name is Vincent and I will be your guide from now until after you are judged. Once you are dressed, we will proceed to the waiting room. I will answer certain questions to the best of my ability and ensure your soul is properly processed."

Walter was listening but was still bewildered by the sudden transition. The newly arrived soul would have to quickly acclimate and accept its circumstances.

"This is not a dream, Mr. Klein. You may choose to believe it is if you like but if you do, I can assure you it is one you will not wake up from anytime soon."

Walter had finished putting on his clothes by the time Vincent completed his explanation. He chose a shirt his wife had designed and made for his 30th birthday. The shirt depicted the scene in the 1986 animated Transformers movie where Optimus Prime lies on his deathbed after Megatron mortally wounds him. The caption below it read, "HE DIED FOR OUR SINS." His wife knew how much he loved Transformers and how strongly he felt about his Atheism, so she jointly expressed these interests in her gift. Walter randomly picked the rest of his articles of clothing: mundane blue jeans and thick white socks. He then sat on his bed to face Vincent.

"So I'm really dead?" said Walter, finally breaking from his stupor.

"I don't think I took away your hearing while I was giving my explanation, did I?"

Walter scrunched his face.

"That was rhetorical. I'm just letting it sink in. Actually, is there a chance I can get a different guide? Some one nicer."

"I'm afraid you're stuck with me, Mr. Klein. I assure you I am only doing this out of duty. If I could choose the souls I guide, I certainly would not have added you to my list."

"Nice to know. And, you might as well call me Walter if we're going to be stuck with each other."

"Very well, Walter. Now, let us proceed to the Waiting Room. You can ask me any other questions you have in a moment."

Vincent opened the bedroom door. Walter was taken aback to see the exit of his bedroom leading to the pathways of Balboa Park in San Diego.

"W-What?" The next transition forced him back into a daze. It felt as if he had died again and fell into some other dimension. Walter knew what he perceived was only an illusion. He told himself repeatedly that he had not just teleported. It was apparent, but his heart needed the repetition so it could scrape against his chest more and more gently until it calmed down. He knew this could not be based in a physical reality, but the stimuli registered the same as when he was alive, making it difficult to adjust.

"Ah Yes. 'Waiting Room' is only a term we use because you and I will be in this area until it is time for your judgment. It's not quite a misnomer. Some Waiting Rooms do actually consist rooms. Remember that none of this is real, Walter," continued Vincent as he saw Walter struggling a bit with the transition.

"Or rather, like the rest of our dimension, none of this exists in a physical plane. The Truth encourages guides to use the example of what you see on a web page in the human realm versus the code that is actually constructing the page. I know you don't have any programming knowledge, so I'll spare you further details of that analogy."

"Yeah, I never understood any of that stuff. Probably best for you to stick with what you were saying before."

"Yes, I know. So as I was saying, The Truth creates a different Waiting Room for each soul. It must've chosen Balboa Park as yours because you have sentiments for the area. It is even possible this Waiting Room was molded from fragments of your memory. I can guarantee you, however, the model The Truth created will feel exactly like the one in the physical realm. You and I are free to enjoy the park until your judgment. I am not to leave your side, but we can do whatever you like otherwise."

Walter turned around to see his apartment had vanished. He was standing next to the fountain adjacent to the science center. The shift gave him another jolt, but he recovered speedily this time now that he was more prepared for such occurrences. Walter reached toward the fountain and felt bits of water splash outside the concrete circle and saturate his hand. The sensation was so accurate. There was nothing fleeting about it. Walter recalled dreams as being like slideshows or old movies flickering on a hand-crank projector. This experience was a high-definition video much too smooth to be a dream.

"This really isn't a dream," said the newly acclimated soul.

The perfectly maintained vividness of his surroundings was what ultimately erased all of Walter's doubts about his situation and assured him Vincent told nothing but the truth. It would be arrogant to think his dreams could create such a world. The stimuli were too rich. Every detail of the fountain was accounted for; every beautiful sign of age, all of its cracks, chips and stains. The pavement in the direction of the wind was wet. More and more drops saturated the ground as the wind blew the descending water away before it could rejoin its next journey through the fountain.

Next to it was the Science Center. Inside there were children playing and parents holding their hands. A small girl was excitedly pressing her fingers onto the electric glass ball and giggling as the current jumped to meet her touch. Her brother was swiping his hands through the air current generated by the wind machine that constantly kept a small ball afloat in midair. The boy was testing himself, seeing if he could move his hand through the airstream without disrupting the ball, a task that required some speed.

Walter sat on the edge of the fountain for a moment and fully accepted his predicament before tapping into his curiosity.

"So I've got tons of questions. When did I die? Was it last night? Was all that stuff, the murdering and everything, just a dream? It felt so real. Shit! I didn't really kill anyone did I?" Walter began to have trouble breathing.

"Don't worry, Walter. What you experienced after Saturday night was a partial cleansing process. None of it happened on the physical plane. It was only designed to feel real. You see, The Truth partially cleanses certain souls so they are easier to process. These souls are usually likely to cause trouble or try to cheat the system. The Truth will normally cleanse a soul who has acted on violence, sexual deviancy or lied excessively during his or her time on Earth. By doing so, The Truth removes this element of their soul so they are unable and unmotivated to disrupt their processing. Other times, partial cleansing is a form of pre-judgment reward, usually for people who were tormented by certain desires but did not sin by acting on them. In your case, The Truth allowed you to experience performing such horrible deeds so you could purge yourself of all the repressed desires you accumulated due to your morbid curiosity. It must've taken pity on you. Also, keep in mind this is different from the complete cleansing that all souls ultimately receive at the end of their journey so they can be fully processed, wiped blank, and recycled. Many souls I've guided confuse the two, so I should mention that."

Walter began to realize the change as Vincent explained the cleansing process. The violent curiosities and dangerous desires were gone. He hadn't once thought about mutilating Vincent for his condescending behavior. The fountain before him was only a fountain. It wasn't a tool for drowning his companion.

"Is that what that guy was; the one who got all up in my mouth?" continued Walter.

"Yes. He was an embodiment of that repression. I believe he began forming around the time you learned of your mother's lover."

Walter's habit of scrunching his face triggered at the thought of that man. He decided to change the subject.

"So I died Saturday night then?"

"Yes. I'm afraid your cancer got the best of you. That tends to happen when you don't treat it."

"How do you know about all of that?"

"I know everything about your life, Walter. Guides have unlimited observational abilities when it comes to the souls they have been tasked with. I watched you allow the cancer to eat away at you. I saw your last expulsion of blood and watched your life ebb away on that bed Saturday night before your cleansing process began."

Walter stared down at the ground as he and Vincent walked along the edge of the fountain.

"I do not mean to shame you, Walter. It is not required of me to judge or question your past actions. My only job is to observe and guide you. I cannot read minds, so I do not know your reasons for refusing treatment. There is also no requirement for you to disclose these reasons to me, although you can if you like."

"Don't worry about me. Anyway, what's this 'Truth' thing you keep mentioning?" Walter was again eager to shift the discussion. He did not yet want to discuss his cancer with Vincent.

"I suppose now is a good time to explain that. No one has a complete understanding of The Truth, but I will tell you everything I know with certainty as well as some speculation my fellow guides and I have. The Truth is a being with nearly absolute power over souls and the spiritual realm. The Truth created the system of spiritual processing you have now become a part of. It may control any soul or being that is part of this dimension. It chooses judges and guides such as myself. The Truth has no power to shape the physical realm. Its observational power, however, is unlimited and exponentially exceeds my own. The Truth can observe any point in history and can watch and process a nearly infinite amount of information."

"Like God?" interrupted Walter.

"I'm surprised to hear such a question from a man who calls himself an Atheist."

"Well doesn't it sound like God?"

"It would behoove you not to think in such terms. The Truth existed long before man invented the idea of 'God.' The Truth also bears no similarity to such a concept because it does not have power over physical substance. The human idea of God does have such powers."

The way Vincent said the word "human" gave Walter pause. He said it like he was referring to a cockroach or some other inferior and disgusting creature.

Walter had assumed that Vincent was another human soul until this point in their journey. Now he began to think that what he perceived only looked human. Walter stared at Vincent while he pondered this until Vincent noticed and glared at him through the corner of his eyes. Walter decided to cut the tension by continuing the conversation.

"Umm… so does that mean God doesn't exist? I don't think it exists, but maybe I can see if I was wrong or not now that I'm dead."

"The Truth has not denounced the idea of another being that created the physical plane in the same manner that The Truth supposedly created the spiritual plane. Nonetheless, the common human idea of God, the kind of God that created man and Earth, is an idea and nothing more. It is something men created to pretend they had knowledge of the universe and an understanding of their species rather than admitting their nescience. It was man's attempt at hiding behind fiction rather than directly confronting the terrifying unknown elements of the world.

"Man, you really don't like humans. Are we really that bad?"

Vincent ignored Walter's bait and continued his explanation of The Truth. For Walter, this was enough to confirm his theory that Vincent wasn't human. Walter wanted to know more on the matter but decided to give it a little more time after seeing Vincent's cold response.

"As I was saying, The Truth processes souls. Perhaps I should explain each step of the process from the beginning so you can have a complete understanding."

"Geez, I thought you've done this a bunch of times."

"Most of the souls I've guided don't ask so many questions nor do they interrupt me so often. Besides, when I said I had guided 'many souls' I only meant one hundred and three. Guiding each soul is a wildly different experience, so I've had difficulty developing a standard protocol." The guide instinctively defended his performance even though he had little pride in his position.

"Sorry." Walter saw Vincent was becoming increasingly annoyed, so he decided to be silent until there was a significant pause in this stage of their journey.

"The process begins when The Truth takes a blank soul and transplants it into a physical body. The interaction between the body and the soul forces the soul to mutate in a unique way, causing each soul to become idiosyncratic. The souls continue to mutate as the body and soul have experience on Earth. Eventually, the body dies and the soul is either partially cleansed before judgment, as yours was, or it is sent directly to its processing journey. In most cases, The Truth guides the soul directly to processing. Guides then take the soul to its Waiting Room where it awaits judgment. During judgment, judges selected by The Truth review the life of the soul on Earth and determine its fate based on factors such as the number of sins committed, the degree of sin, whether or not punishment was received on Earth and many other factors. Similar to the law of man, sins are judged more severely if they inflict damage to others and not only to the self. The Truth would surely convict a man who sells drugs more harshly than a man who buys drugs deemed illegal under the law of man. Nonetheless, sins such as adultery, excessive and selfish lying and torture during war, which man's law does not necessarily punish in many societies, are judged here as if they were in violation of a generally agreed upon set of laws. The criterion varies between judges. All judges, however, decide whether each soul loses the 'Right of Choice' or retains it. Judges can also dole out a punishment before revoking rights. The Right of Choice allows worthy souls to choose between non-existence and a period of simulated reality before the soul is completely cleansed and recycled. The Truth prescribes the simulated reality, which is usually pleasurable for the worthy soul. For example, a worthy handicapped man I guided received a simulation where he was allowed to live a life with use of his legs while retaining memories of his life without the use of his legs. Generally speaking, souls cannot create their own fantasy. The Truth leaves only the most worthy of souls with the option of customizing a fantasy or post-processing journey. After the simulation is over, the soul is completely cleansed and recycled. As for those who choose non-existence, I obviously cannot say what happens to them. Few choose this option."

Walter felt a bit overwhelmed. It was a lot of information for any one person to process. Still, there were details that stood out to him.

"So what are my chances of keeping this Right of Choice thing?"

"I cannot say with certainty. Normally, souls that receive partial cleansing before their judgment do not retain their Right of Choice. The Truth often cleanses serial killers and other dangerous psychotics before they are assigned a guide. This makes potentially dangerous souls easier to guide and process. I have, however, heard of souls being partially cleansed and still retaining their Right of Choice. The cleansing process is not always successful because The Truth is an admittedly imperfect being."

"Great. So I get lumped in with serial killers," said a crestfallen and sarcastic Walter.

"I wasn't implying that. I am only telling you what I know."

"I know. I didn't mean to sound upset. It just doesn't look good for me. Are they gonna judge me on all that stuff I did during the cleansing?"

"They will not. You did not actually commit any of those crimes in the physical realm."

"Yeah but wouldn't it look bad to the judge because I wanted to do all that stuff?"

"It does not matter. A good man is merely one who has the will to defy or ignore urges to commit crimes society deems cruel or unacceptable. Both 'good' and 'bad' men, as humans call them, have the same potential for horrific action. The choice to tap into this potential is what differentiates the two. A good man has the willpower and conviction to ignore his maladaptive urges while generally behaving positively and considerately. The Truth does not judge thoughts of sin, only actions. We do not deem it fair to judge a man's desires and curiosities. The act or lack thereof is all that matters."

"OK I get it. I guess I'm lucky then." Walter didn't realize he had interrupted. Vincent aggressively talked over him, his voicing rising and drowning out Walter's fleeting comment.

"I learned this when I guided a man who was sexually attracted to children during his time in the physical realm. He was judged excellently because he had not acted on these urges and had suffered much as a result. The Truth prescribed the San Diego Children's Museum as his Waiting Room and generated a fantasy world where it was not illegal or even frowned upon to have sexual relations with children. He also experienced an orgy with numerous children of both genders during his cleansing process. I enjoyed this man's company. He was quiet and didn't ask so many questions, definitely one of my favorite souls. My point, though, is that being partially cleansed before judgment doesn't necessarily mean you are doomed to be harshly judged. The part of the soul The Truth cleanses is often a part that burdens its owner, a part the owner might wish to empty himself of. Perhaps I misspoke earlier."

Walter headed to the Museum of Man. The idea of satisfying pedophiles and rewarding them in the afterlife disturbed Walter. He assuaged this feeling by trusting that all of these experiences were created harmlessly and that actual children weren't used in the fantasies. If his hunch about the park being constructed from his favorite memories was true, he knew the mummy exhibit would be showing. Walter was happy to see the Egyptian banner outside of the museum. He clambered up the stairs like a giddy child.

"So what are they going to judge me on then?" Walter had to raise his voice as he and Vincent toured the crowded museum from Walter's memory of the opening.

"Most likely the incident with your mother's lover." Walter nearly choked on his overpriced, museum bought soda after hearing this. He began dreading his judgment and searched for something to trigger a subject change so he could ease his mind. The soul also disapproved of the word "lover" because he was almost certain his mother had not consummated her relationship with that man. After looking at the marvelously preserved bodies for a couple of minutes, Walter realized he had forgotten an important question.

"Hey, Vincent. What happened to my body? How long has it been since I died?"

"Human conceptions of time are of little consequence in this dimension. Nonetheless, I can tell you what happened to your body."

"Go ahead."

"Your body lay in bed for several days until it began to smell. Your neighbor smelled something foul coming from your home, but he did not investigate for another day."

"OK, that's enough."

"The smell becomes increasingly strong, so your neighbor knocks on the door. He receives no answer and eventually calls the police."

"All right, that's not exactly what I wanted to know. That's not what I meant."

"The police come in and find your corpse on the bed."

"That's enough!"

"Why are you upset, Walter? I am answering your question."

"Look, I didn't want to know about all the rotting and gross stuff. I meant what happens at my funeral?"

"You should have been more specific. I assumed from your reaction to the mummies that you wanted to know those kinds of details."

"I'm sorry. Can you please tell me what happens at my funeral?" said Walter with mock politeness.

Vincent paused for a moment. His eyes rolled around and twitched as if he were searching through a database located in the back of his skull. This nauseated Walter. He turned his head away while Vincent's eyes showed white. After a few seconds, they rolled back into place and the brown pupils resurfaced.

"Fifty-seven people attend your funeral. It takes place in the church where you married your wife. Several of your friends and members of your wife's family speak about you. Your friends talk about your kindness and share anecdotes. Your wife's family talks about their respect for you and how amazed they were when you lifted your wife out of her depression."

"Is any of my family there?"

"No."

"Oh. Not even Mom?"

"No."

"Why not?"

"I cannot say. I can only observe."

Walter sat on a museum bench and stared at the ground before continuing. He hadn't expected his mother to be there, but the confirmation was still hurtful.

"Are Kyle and the guys there?"

"Yes. They each talk about you. I can read the transcripts if you like."

"It's OK, you don't have to tell me all of it. It was all nice stuff though, right?"

"Yes, they had nothing but kind words for you."

Walter began traveling toward one of his favorite parts of the park with Vincent in tow, walking a few paces behind, calmly following and observing him. Along the way, Walter studied the objects around him with envy, wishing he could be as brimming with life, color and expression.

The vibrancy never extinguished. It only fluctuated between dim and brilliant because San Diego, like most of Southern California, was nearly devoid of seasons. More specifically, he admired beautiful objects that could stand on their own. Public art was his favorite, which was why he was journeying to the western side of the park where the statue of Kate Sessions stood.

Historians often referred to Kate Sessions as the "Mother of Balboa Park." Sessions had planted a significant portion of the trees that still stood tall in the park and in many other areas of San Diego. She leased the land from the city so she could do so. The successful and kind woman did not marry during her eighty-two years of life. She was rich, accomplished, loved, memorialized and alone even in her post-mortem incarnation.

The humble grey statue of this woman stood out in the midst of floral earth, beaming with pride and modest beauty. A portion of the soil that had given birth to the park was in her left hand, her potting tool in the other. Even if the flowers around her wilted and the earth dried up, they would not diminish her elegance. If the government leveled the land, someone would surely fight to keep her standing or perhaps uproot her and steal her away to reside somewhere else.

Walter could not empathize with this woman despite his admiration. He formed his greatest bond with the idea of the stones surrounding a keystone. There were terms for these stones such as "voussoirs" and "springers." The humble widower didn't use them, though, because he thought they made such stones sound more important and unique than they actually were. Those stones had no function before they were placed with the keystone. Some were built specifically to support that special one at the top of the arch. If someone removed the keystone or if some cruel force knocked it asunder, the adjacent stones would surely fall. In the worst of cases, the falling stones would crumble and become useless. Those stones had to continue existing even after their purpose was gone.

Walter and Vincent left the museum and headed for the koi pond. Walter felt a chill and a film in his eyes as he saw a couple with their newborn son. They were young, foolish and full of happiness. The baby dabbled his hands in the koi pond and laughed at the fish. The mother said "No" until he cried, so now she held him by his ribs and let him touch the pond while the rolls of baby fat pressed themselves between her fingers. And there was the father, dressed in uniform. He was shipping out to fight in Vietnam the next day.

Walter's father, Eugene, hated his name. Despite his gentle nature, he thought Eugene sounded like the kind of name a weak man would have. He insisted that everyone call him Gene to the point where only his wife and the government knew his real name. Walter heard about it when his mother got drunk, which was incredibly rare even though she worked at many bars.

"Your son's adorable," said Walter as he approached Eugene.

"Thanks."

"I'm W-Will by the way." Walter nearly bit his lip to stop himself from saying his real name.

"Gene." The two men shook hands. Walter made sure his shake was firm before continuing the conversation.

"So when do you ship out, if you don't mind me asking?"

"Oh I don't mind. I ship out tomorrow actually."

"I hope I'm not interrupting anything." He said it a bit coyly, but not with enough inflection for Eugene to detect.

"Don't worry about it. It'll be another ten minutes at least before my son gets bored with that pond."

Walter looked over to see himself as a baby. He'd forgotten how fat he was and how much his mother worried about him not losing the baby weight.

"Don't you get worried?" asked Walter, giving his father a solemn look.

"About what?"

"Not coming back."

39

"Well, I'm a sniper, so there isn't so much risk for guys like me."

Walter produced a sad, grim laugh. The irony was irresistible.

"What's so funny?"

"Oh nothing," said Walter, attempting to stifle his chuckling.

Walter felt a hand on his shoulder.

"We should go now," said Vincent.

Walter nodded and looked back at his father before leaving.

"It was nice meeting you, Eugene."

Walter had wanted to address his father that way.

The atmosphere blurred and distorted as if someone had a knob and was turning down the number of pixels available in the world.

"Wait, we're going to judgment now?"

"Yes, where did you think we were going?"

"I thought you just meant we had to keep wandering around the Waiting Room. Man, there was so much more stuff I wanted to see and do: The Zoo, the train. Oh man they probably had festivals and fireworks since it was generated from my memories."

"Sorry, Walter. You're being called for judgment. It's your time."

"I thought you said we didn't have to worry about time here."

"I said the concept of time is different. Time exists differently here than it does in the physical plane. Don't mince my words."

Walter saw Vincent becoming agitated again, so he stopped complaining.

"Alright, fine. Can I ask you one more question? I think it'll be my last one for a while. I promise."

"You should ask now. This might be your last chance."

"Alright then. Are you human?"

"I am not. I am a purely spiritual being."

"Why do you look like a regular person then?"

"My form appears human because this is what you are able to perceive. Nonetheless, I am not a human anymore."

"Anymore?"

"Yes. I was once human. The Truth chose my soul to become a guide and forced me to transcend humanity and become a superior being."

"You think you're better than humans?"

"I think spiritual beings are superior to humans in both their physical and spiritual forms. We do not require food, water, sleep or any form of nourishment humans need. We are incapable of sin. We also have superior observational abilities and a pure form humans cannot achieve in the spiritual realm."

"Well, you may think that's great, but I'd be miserable if I couldn't eat or drink anything. I mean, don't you remember what it was like to be human? Don't you miss those things sometimes?"

"I do not need to answer these questions. They have nothing to do with your judgment and I have already gone beyond my duties in answering your other questions. Besides, we are about to arrive."

Part 3

One

The Balboa Park koi pond continued to distort and dissolve, making Walter nauseous. The entrance to a courtroom materialized in its place. The spiritual beings referred to it as a "courtroom," but its appearance was an odd cross between an amphitheater, a coliseum and a courtroom.

The sign above the courtroom double doors read "IN" on the right side and "Waiting Room" on the left. Vincent opened the right hand door and ushered Walter in. Walter's eyes widened at the sight of the bustling courtroom. There were hardwood floors and bleachers with leather cushions reclining, and generous legroom on both sides of the court. Both stands had ten rows arranged so everyone had a clear view of the courtroom floor and the judge's stand. Four alabaster columns supported the roof without obscuring any desirable views.

There was a marble wall behind the judge with statements carved into it. The statements were numbered and began on the top left corner. The numbers increased as they went down the wall from top to bottom and then shifted to the next column. Each column expanded to fit the width of the statement, almost like an Excel spreadsheet. There was still space on the wall and the last column wasn't filled. Some of the previous statements had been crossed out. It was a like a living document.

Walter scanned the wall and read some of the statements as Vincent guided him to the left-hand bleachers.

34. Despair to the adulterers
43. Despair to the arrogant

79. Despair to those who falsify the truth and force it upon others
99. Joy to those who have never known it
154. Joy to the selfless
169. Despair to the violators

Behind the judge's stand in the northwest corner of the room was a tall wooden door with the label "Secondary Waiting Room." The northeast corner was the same and maintained the symmetrical pattern of the courtroom. Its label read "Post-Judgment."

Walter could see mouths moving on the bleachers but couldn't hear anything until he passed a thin line carved into the floor. The line was carved around both sets of bleachers in a rectangle. The moment he crossed it, a soft cacophony of mutterings resounded off invisible walls. It startled him for a moment.

"Do not worry, Walter. There is a sound barrier in the bleachers so souls and guides may converse without interrupting the judgment."

"Hey, Vince. Over here."

A guide named Francis shouted this from the ninth row. He wore casual clothing and had his assigned soul seated next to him. Francis was an alternative energy salesman during his human life and hadn't been a guide nearly as long as Vincent. Vincent spotted him and then ushered Walter up to the ninth row.

"Hi, I'm Francis," said the guide, extending his hand to Walter.

"Nice to meet you."

"Why don't you sit here? It's good for souls to interact with each other a bit before they get judged." Francis motioned his hand to a small space between himself and his assigned soul. He scooted over as he instructed Walter to sit, making space for the two souls to sit together. Vincent sat on the edge of the row next to Francis. There was enough space for the pair of souls and the pair of guides to have their respective private conversations.

Francis and Vincent didn't have frequent interactions, so they were happy to see each other. The congregation was a pleasant surprise because it was difficult for guides to arrange meetings and hangouts; their schedules were all so different. They both perceived the other as a confidante and intellectual equal despite their polar mannerisms and beliefs. Each meeting had rich conversation: critiquing the spiritual system, debating which sins were deserving of which punishments, discussing the nature of The Truth and all the human behavior they found most interesting and amusing. Oddly enough, their polar attitudes toward humanity and the spiritual processing system were what bonded them so quickly.

"How's it going, Vince?" asked Francis.

"Well. And yourself?" replied Vincent.

"I'm good, I'm good. So how's your human this time around?"

"He's an interesting man. He can be insolent at times but I can generally tolerate his company."

"Why do you think The Truth placed him with you?"

"It's probably due to our similar attitudes in the physical realm regarding loved ones."

"That's it?" exclaimed Francis "A lot of the other guides are gossiping about how The Truth gave you a Special Focus soul. I thought you'd have something more interesting to say about him."

"I assumed he would be more intriguing as well," replied Vincent. "He hasn't had any notable accomplishments on Earth. Even his violent urges are not that rare. There must be something I'm missing."

"Give it your best try. Maybe you'll get that meeting with The Truth you've been wanting. Speaking of which, how's that going?"

"Not well." Vincent's tone became more bitter than usual. "I haven't been able to communicate with it. As time trudges on, The Truth reminds me more and more of the God humans created and wrote about in the Old Testament: arrogant, sadistic, manipulative, taking great pleasure in demonstrating his power and teaching lessons that make little sense, in short: an asshole."

Francis laughed heartily. Some of the other guides and souls noticed and turned their heads for a moment.

"I'm glad to see you haven't changed since the last time we chatted," said Francis. Vincent blushed slightly and decided to change the subject.

"What about you? Have you been enjoying your most recent soul?"

"He's a good guy, not perfect of course but I'll be sad to see him go."

"You don't think he'll retain his Right of Choice?"

"Probably not. I guess I shouldn't get attached."

"Becoming attached to humans is a waste of time in my opinion."

"Yeah yeah, I know. You've said that before. I can't help it, though. I've seen this guy through every step of his life. I can still remember the day he was born, when his soul fluttered in there, newly mutated, ready to begin its journey. It's kind of like watching a TV series and then seeing your favorite character die at the end. Really tugs at the heart strings, man."

"Televisions hadn't been invented during my supposed past life as a human," Vincent responded coldly.

Francis was silent for a while after he saw that his usual attempt to make Vincent more sympathetic to humans was only aggravating him. The way Vincent used the word "supposed" showed he still hated The Truth. Vincent hoped The Truth had fabricated his memories of his human life and that he had not actually been human. He refused to believe he could have been part of such a species. The bitter guide had no way of proving his theory, though. He wanted to ask The Truth several questions: "Are all guides crafted from human souls? Have you inserted artificial memories into any guides? What is your rationale for our current system? Have you considered making any changes? How long do I have to serve as a guide?"

"How have your ambitions progressed since the last time we spoke?" continued Vincent.

"It's hard to tell. All of the judges I've talked to said it came out of nowhere when they got their promotions. It seems likely I'll get it, though." Francis did not mention that he briefly spoke with The Truth so he could avoid making Vincent jealous.

Francis had his own theories about enigmatic elements of the spiritual processing system. He believed The Truth was a mantle that high-ranking spiritual beings took up for a period of time, much like a presidential term. In the spiritual realm, hard-working guides were often promoted to judges. The Truth then promoted some judges to arch guides, beings that were rumored to have the ability to travel through time and space as invisible and intangible ghosts in the physical realm. These arch guides could bring the most incredible and deserving human souls with them if they wished. Arch guides also had the power to assist The Truth in granting customized fantasies to amazing and selfless souls, an ability other spiritual beings had personally confirmed. These experiences were vastly superior to the prescribed fantasies most souls received because The Truth and the arch guide allowed the soul to assist in crafting the experience.

None of the guides knew what happened to arch guides after they finished serving. It seemed they disappeared or were processed so their spiritual material could be recycled and reused later. Francis, however, was sure these guides became The Truth before being completely processed. To him, it explained why the spiritual system had a history of undergoing occasional and sudden restructurings. Each new taker of the mantle would surely have a different vision for what the spiritual realm should be like. Francis wanted to be the next in this line of beings, were they to exist. After becoming a judge, he would strive for a promotion to arch guide, hoping to confirm the time travel ability for himself. Then, following another promotion, he would take the mantle and become the best arbiter in the history of the spiritual realm. These were his ambitions. He had not been able to ask The Truth about it but still remained hopeful.

Both guides looked at one another and realized there was nothing more to say. Francis was beginning to believe that he might never save his friend from the quagmire of bitterness that currently enveloped him. They remained silent and looked to their souls, wondering what the other pair might be discussing.

The soul Francis was guiding was a physical masterpiece of a man. He had broad shoulders and a thin waist, a gentle jaw and smooth hair that bristled perfectly as it meshed with the bit of gel holding it up in the front. His muscles appeared as if someone had drawn them. There were no noticeable imperfections in his form.

Because Walter had been reading *Death in Venice* shortly before his own demise, the way he observed his fellow soul reminded him a bit of how the aging Aschenbach had gazed upon young Tadzio. The fascination was not sexual. Walter studied him like a piece in a museum, one that consumed his time in the place even though he had paid admission to see all of the collection, a piece so finely crafted that to dismiss it would be an insult to the artist and the forces of luck that had combined to create it.

When Walter saw people like this soul, he thought of some of the ideas he had of God when he was younger. The staunch Atheist never believed in God, but he loved entertaining the idea and fantasizing about how God might use its abilities. He thought about God much the way a boy would imagine a superhero or a mythical creature. Physical beauty triggered this because Walter imagined God standing next to a conveyor belt with lumps of flesh strolling by on their way to a machine that would determine their features as an adult. This machine was randomized to give the bodies adequately attractive features taken from their parents. Nonetheless, God might remove one of these lumps from the belt on occasion if it was feeling inspired. It would then craft this lump with all its power so the physical form would someday approach perfection.

Walter also knew appraisals of physical worth were subjective. His thoughts went back to his wife, as they always did, and he ruminated on how he perceived her to be the most beautiful being in existence. He romanticized the notion that God created people for one another when he thought of her. Yet, he realized she was not objectively as attractive as he perceived her to be. The widower could not remember a single time where a friend or family member had described her as attractive. Was it the splash of deformities that consumed her neck and licked the bottom of her chin, putting the area in sharp contrast with the smooth and tinted skin on the rest of her body? Walter fell deeper into this daydream as he conjured a memory on the subject.

"That stuff on your neck is a part of you and it's beautiful because you're beautiful as a whole. I love it along with rest."

He didn't have the most elegant way of articulating his affection.

"Hey, I'm David." The invitation for dialogue pulled Walter out of his thoughts. He felt guilty after realizing he had been awkwardly sitting silent for a minute or so.

"Walter," he responded, extending his arm for a shake.

"How have you been handling this whole system so far?" David out-stretched his hand and made an odd motion as he said the word "system." It was as if he were sprinkling something across the courtroom, hoping a wind would catch it and expand its area of effect.

"It's been strange but not so bad," replied Walter. "I'm mostly glad the cleansing process is over."

"Oh you got put through that, too. You're the first person I've talked to up here who also had a cleansing process. How was yours?"

Walter mused upon how David said "up here" as if they were in heaven, in the clouds. The Atheist hesitated to answer the question, though, looking down in shame for a moment instead.

"Oh, I'm sorry, man," said David. "I didn't mean to press so hard. You don't have to talk about if you don't want to."

"No, it's OK. I didn't do those things after all."

"I murdered a few people," continued Walter after another pause. He couldn't bring himself to mention the rape for some reason. He wondered if it was because he considered it worse somehow than murder. Certainly the legal system on Earth implied that murder was a more severe crime since it meant taking a life. People survived after being sexually assaulted but, at least in Walter's mind, the crime was more heinous since it forced the victim to live forever with the memory of the violation.

"Man, you must've been holding a lot back."

"I was. What about you? What was your cleansing process like?"

Like Walter, David hesitated.

"Oh come on, man. I told you mine," said Walter, becoming more comfortable.

"You're right. You're right," said David with a smile. "I won't blue ball you. Fair is fair."

Walter smiled as well. He liked the way David talked. The honesty, vulgar but endearing language, and mannerisms; the accessible nature at odds with such an elite form, all reminded him a bit of his mother. Both men began to believe they would've been good friends had they met before death.

"I really like women a lot… or at least fucking them. During my cleansing process, I got invited to this thing called… 'Pussy Fest." David blushed as he finished the sentence. The sheer ridiculousness of the name made it hard to say with a straight face.

Walter chuckled. "You didn't think that was suspicious?"

"You know how it was, man. If yours was the same as mine, you couldn't think about whether or not things made sense. You just went with it."

Walter recalled his cleansing process and realized David was correct. There was no remorse, no hesitation or questioning the ridiculousness of it all. Yet it felt real, like it *could* realistically happen given some stroke of luck bestowed only once in a lifetime.

"Anyway, yeah I accepted the invitation and showed up there," continued David. "It was crazy, this huge mansion with women I always wanted to meet like Kate Upton, all the Victoria's Secret models, even older ladies I used to fantasize about like Heidi Klum. I got to fuck every single one of them."

"That's pretty awesome," replied Walter. "Definitely way better than my cleansing process."

"I feel so different. I haven't even looked at a woman since I got here. Oddly enough, I really like it. Feels like I'm the kind of person I wanted to be."

"You didn't want to be getting laid all the time?" said Walter coyly, beginning to form enough of a rapport with David so he thought he could joke around.

"Not if it meant hurting my wife." David's tone became solemn.

"Oh I see. She meant a lot to you."

"She did. That woman changed my life for the better, taught me to believe. I told her my body and soul were hers forever under the eyes of God. I only gave her the latter half, though. Even as I was saying it, I knew I would only be able to keep the first part of that promise."

"So you cheated on her a lot?"

The faithful widower tried to erase the judgment and condemnation in his voice. His instinct was to attack people's religious beliefs, especially when they clashed with the person's life decision and created hypocrisy. David made him think of his mother, though, and his mother had taught him to be tolerant, which was wise as a minority in a thoroughly religious world. Besides, he liked David for the most part, at least so far.

"Yeah I did," responded David with palpable remorse. "People scoff at sex addiction like it's not a real thing, but I knew I had it. Got diagnosed and everything. I guess that's no excuse, though."

Given how David looked, Walter understood how he would be able to maintain such an addiction. David's addiction actually had some similar roots to Walter's violent desires. It was curiosity. David wanted to know how each different woman would react, what sounds she might make, how soon she would climax, what she would do for him without asking.

"Would you mind if I asked you something that might offend you a little?" said Walter.

"Go for it."

"Why bother with religion and God if you're going to sin like that? I just don't understand."

David laughed. "You're not religious are you?"

Walter didn't like how David was trying to deflect the question, but the polite thing to do was answer.

"I'm an Atheist."

David finally noticed Walter's shirt and its religious mockery. He smiled and continued his inquiry.

"So you never went to church?"

"Nope. Not really."

"See, that's why you don't understand. Being part of a religious community isn't just about the beliefs. Sometimes it has very little to do with that. Most religious people I knew didn't pay attention to even half the stuff in the Bible. How could they? Who wants to wait until marriage to have sex? Not me, man."

Before continuing, he paused for a moment and looked up at the courtroom ceiling like he was gazing at some far away mountain. It was his attempt to look into the past and focus so he could properly answer Walter's question.

"Before I met my wife and started going to church, I never thought anyone could love me. I believed in God already, but I hated him. I got abused a lot as a kid, tormented even, used like a dishrag and then thrown out. I thought it was all God's fault. I thought it was his responsibility to protect me because he's so powerful. When I met my wife, she started taking me to church and showed me that people could be kind and accepting. I made friends with decent people for the first time. I started believing in God again in a positive way because she helped me understand him differently. I was so happy. As for the cheating, I really thought God was gonna punish me. I wished everyday he would stop me or strike me down so I wouldn't feel so guilty. I guess he kind of did in the end. He works in mysterious ways as they say…as my wife used to say."

Both men were silent for a moment as they reflected upon their former lives and the ideals they still carried with them.

"How does it feel to know you were wrong about the afterlife?" David managed to say this without hostility despite the nature of the question. Walter could tell he was simply looking for something to continue the conversation.

"It's strange. I'm not upset per se, but I am surprised. I really did think there was nothing after I died. Wouldn't it be more upsetting for you, though? This place isn't even remotely close to the Christian vision of heaven. Where you end up isn't a shared space. There are no clouds, no angels, no nothing."

"I didn't really think heaven would be like that. I think people just romanticize all the angels and clouds and everything. I'm only interested in meeting God." He said it with such hope, like it was destined to happen.

At first, Walter considered reminding him of how likely that was. The idea of meeting God was intriguing, though. "What would you do if you met him?" asked Walter.

"I have a lot of questions for him. 'How much power do you have? How much have you done so far? Can I atone for what I did to my wife?" David said this last question softly.

"I hope you can," replied Walter. "I think most people should get a chance to do the right thing."

"Thanks, man. I hope so too."

A thud like the sound of a watermelon dropping from a building startled Walter and disrupted the conversation. Walter stood and looked to the side of the bleachers to see a pool of blood emanating from a nun's head. She had jumped off the bleachers and, with practice, attempted suicide in a way where her head would strike the ground with full force. David was horrified, on the verge of having tears stain his perfect form. Vincent was disgusted and annoyed for a moment before he feigned indifference. Francis became upset and rose from his seat.

"All right. Whose soul is that?"

"I'm so sorry, Francis." A timid and newly appointed guide wearing a tuxedo scurried down the bleachers to the nun's body. His name was Brett.

"Why didn't you stop her?" barked Francis.

"I tried. She promised she wouldn't do it again. I shouldn't have believed her I guess," replied Brett.

"No shit."

Francis towered over Brett. He crossed his arms as he knelt next to the nun's body. Brett placed his hand over her head and the blood that had spattered on the ground levitated and poured back into place. To Walter, it almost appeared as if time was being reversed in a process localized to the nun. The cracks in her skull and bruises on her body healed and Brett brought her to her feet. It was as if Brett was denying the event had happened.

"How'd he do that?" Walter asked a mentally aloof Vincent.

Vincent did not feel like answering more questions. Nonetheless, he remembered the code The Truth specified and knew, unlike some of Walter's other questions, this was one he had to answer.

"Souls can be damaged, but guides have the ability to heal them. Everything we experience here is a perception created by The Truth using the physical realm as a reference point because all of us originate from there. Think of the blood you are seeing as more of a representation of some kind of spiritual injury she is attempting to inflict on herself. There is no serious danger. It is merely an annoyance from an ignorant and stubborn human."

Walter constructed this woman's story as he watched her. He could only imagine how hard it would be to live life as a nun with an unwavering belief in God only to discover that even the afterlife did not contain evidence of his existence. He could tell by looking at her that she was a thorough believer. She had read the Bible hundreds of times.

Once she was on her feet, Francis plunged his fingers into her chest. There were some gasps in the bleachers. His fingers penetrated her flesh without any blood or injury. There was a refined technique in how he did it without mutilating her. The skin and tissue gave way and rippled outwards as if Francis had transmuted it into water. She stopped struggling after he did this. He forced her into docility much like Vincent had done to Walter. His fingers were syringes full of morphine.

"Just do that if she gets crazy again," Francis shouted to Brett as he returned to his seat. Brett hung his head as he escorted the nun up the bleachers.

"Fuckin' newbies, man," hissed Francis as he plopped down next to Walter and Vincent. "He's embarrassing us in front of the judge. The Truth could be checking this out too."

"It's not entirely his fault," responded Vincent. "It seems The Truth tasked him with a particularly difficult soul."

The nun's name was Yolanda Smith. She had a domineering Mexican mother who insisted on the first name. Her White father yielded easily, afraid his wife would leave after the smallest conflict. He was happy to have a beautiful woman, considering how he looked. They were wonderful parents and raised her well.

Unfortunately remnants of a violent anti-Catholic organization butchered them. These murderous bigots believed Yolanda's light-skinned Catholic family was part of the lingering stench of the Spanish clergy. After this Yolanda dedicated herself to God. She worked tirelessly and became the Mother Superior of a convent in Tijuana.

God would protect. God would shelter her from the horrors that roamed in the world he created. God would reward her for her lack of sin when her heart stopped beating.

She lived happily in the convent until she developed a heart condition she had no money to treat. It took her life as she was dragging a wooden cross through the aisle of the church. She collapsed on the cross and did not make it to the ground. They held each other in equilibrium. Both refused to yield.

"David Peretti!" shouted the judge.

The announcement startled David and awoke him from deep thoughts. Walter could tell watching the nun's despair had shaken his resolve a little or at least challenged his faith. He was witnessing divergent paths of two people faced with the same harsh possibility that all of their beliefs were completely unfounded. The nun saw the existence of the spiritual plane as evidence against God. She thought it disproved much of what she had devoted her life to. In her mind, there was no God because she surely would have met him soon after death. On the other hand, David still believed. He perceived the soul processing system as another step before his encounter with the true afterlife and the God he had hoped for. What he was experiencing now was merely a test of faith, a strange purgatory acting as a barrier between him and the world he had imagined. There was no telling who would be right or wrong. Even The Truth could not deny the idea of God. It could only tell souls it could not offer them any evidence of God.

The two men's eyes met as David rose and began to exit the bleachers. They merely nodded and shook hands again. No words passed between them. The perfectly-crafted man approached the stand and joined Francis, ready to accept his fate, still hopeful that his journey was not about to end.

"We have time for one little trial before we get to the big one. They're late so I might as well pass time while we wait." The judge muttered this as he shuffled through his desk and watched Francis and David move towards him.

"Mr. Peretti, you did not accomplish much of significance on Earth," began the judge. "You did considerable charity work through your church. You also cheated on your wife many times. I suppose her stabbing you to death was punishment enough, so I won't give you another one during your soul processing."

Walter realized what David had meant when he implied that God had indirectly punished him for his infidelity. He pitied the man. Even for Walter, such a death would have been too painful to imagine.

"However," continued the judge, "you will not retain your right of choice. You will proceed immediately to nothingness. That is all."

Francis guided David back to the bleachers. He could have fully processed him rather than prolonging his now humiliating stay in the courtroom. The guide refused to miss the upcoming trial, though. He would not take the chance. David was battered but still hopeful he might meet God after the processing was over. He took his seat with Francis in the first row, out of Walter's sight.

Only David's adultery, grizzly death and charity work had made it to the trial. The abuses he had suffered, the mental and emotional growth he achieved after meeting his wife, the friends he made, his career, the beautiful words he said to his wife; the judge had silently and invisibly calculated these aspects before the trial.

Showing them would not be as entertaining, though, not as juicy. Spiritual beings didn't want to sit through an excruciatingly detailed autobiography of a man they judged as common and boring. The Truth knew this and made an effort to distill the facts of the soul's life on Earth down to a few heavy drops that would be served to the judge. Once the judge had this information, he or she decided what to do with the soul. Most of the process was something The Truth could execute on its own. One of the great merits of its system, however, was that it deceived man into thinking only beings who were once men were judging them.

The Truth was not authoritarian, though. Guides could argue against the judge if they believed their soul was about to be processed unjustly. The Truth rarely interfered. It allowed the judge to come to his or her own decision, which meant seniority and rank triumphed if the judge and guide disagreed on a soul's fate.

The brevity and nature of the trial shocked Walter. He thought back to the first time he watched the original version of *12 Angry Men* with his wife. The movie was about a jury of men deliberating the guilt of a young Latino man who had allegedly murdered his father. His wife had been nagging him to watch it with her for a few days.

"It sounds really boring. It's just guys sitting in a room and talking right?"

"Oh my God, Walt, you're such a typical guy when it comes to movies. You don't want to see it unless it has big tits and explosions in it."

"I don't need to watch a movie to see that first one."

"You're not gonna see them tonight if you don't watch the Henry Fonda movie with me. Come on, it's a classic!"

Though Walter was resistant at first, he was glad his wife had gotten him to see it in the end. He learned that time itself was a form of respect and humanization when it came to deciding the fate of another member of the species. No matter how obvious the verdict, no matter how much evidence weighed toward guilty or not guilty, the case had to be discussed. Whether it was a boy from a slum or a famous music producer from Hollywood, whether the case was a microcosm of larger issues and controversial laws or a simple theft, the court had to give it time and thorough discussion. To do less than that was to throw away a life as if it belonged to an animal that possessed no understanding of justice and equality.

Walter turned to Vincent. The cleansing had stifled the ability to feel anger and violence. Still, his voice reflected how much the system was offending him.

"How much of this is necessary?" asked Walter.

"What do you mean?"

"This! All of this!" exclaimed Walter as he motioned his hand around the courtroom. "Is it actually necessary for the processing?"

"It depends on your opinion."

Vincent's response irritated Walter. It reminded him of the kind of answer a politician would give: words strung together to produce nothing, words existing only to fill time, make sound and placate if they were lucky. Vincent continued upon seeing how dissatisfied Walter was with his initial response.

"It depends on what you think the purpose of this courtroom is. Is it necessary for processing the soul? Of course not. The Truth could do most of this by itself or leave it to only a guide and a judge. Only a fool would value it in that way. Is it necessary for allowing us purely spiritual beings to reflect on our former existence and make our time serving as guides more bearable? In this case, the answer is a resounding 'Yes.'"

Walter craned his neck so he could try and spot David. He then rose and made his way to the bottom of the bleachers. His fellow soul and budding friend needed compassion. Without rising himself, Vincent grabbed Walter's wrist and restrained him. His movements were not forceful, but the grip was powerful. Walter tried briefly to break from it but was not able to budge his hand even a millimeter. It was strange to feel the cold from Vincent's touch. The skin seemed at least somewhat artificial, nearly devoid of striations, wrinkles and blemishes. Walter realized it was different than David's hand. He thought about what Vincent had said earlier, how everything he was experiencing and absorbing with his five senses was a representation of spiritual matter. He wondered if the subtle differences in Vincent's form represented his superior strength as a guide. He wondered if souls were capable of resisting and harnessing the kind of spiritual power guides possessed.

"Sit down, Walter. The next trial is about to begin. It would not be wise for you to disturb it."

Walter felt the threat and hostility in Vincent's words even though the tone was flat. The powerless soul took his seat slowly and Vincent released his arm. Walter realized he would not be able to make his way down the bleachers at that moment, at least not without getting in trouble. Murmurs and mumblings filled the room. The guides were impatient. They were waiting for something.

For the first time since Vincent explained the spiritual processing system, Walter thought about what he would do if he retained his Right of Choice. He was beginning to further understand the value of a prescribed fantasy and what some souls would want The Truth to give them. They yearned for a second life, whether it was a chance for redemption or an opportunity to relive the best pleasures of their former lives. Walter had regrets and would surely make some different choices if The Truth allowed him an experience where he could retain his old memories and start over around the time his relationship with his mother started deteriorating. He would have another shot at finding passion in his career instead of only in his relationship with his wife. But did he really want this, or was guilt the only source of motivation?

Watching David also made him realize he had not failed in every aspect of his life. He had succeeded in making his wife happier than she was before they met. As a husband, he had no regrets.

Two

Another guide entered the courtroom with her soul. The soul was a man with a capital "T" branded into his forehead. This signified that he was a top priority, much higher than Walter.

"It's time to be silent and watch," said Vincent with a whisper of excitement.

"Hey, shut the fuck up, everyone!" shouted a clearly excited Francis.

All of the guides instructed their souls to be quiet. All eyes were on the new soul. The judge rose from his seat and raised his hand to further cement the silence.

The soul was a frightening man. He was more than six feet tall and had a wide neck rippling with muscle. His baggy jeans and loose black shirt failed to hide his muscular form. His bald scalp gleamed in the courtroom light. The contrasts made it look as if his little eyes were pushed far back into his enormous head. His mouth and nose appeared as if a miniature black hole inside his skull were attempting to swallow these features. His presence cracked through the air, and he smiled as his guide led him down the courtroom floor in chains. Even the specs of dust and dirt on the floor scurried away, seeking shelter behind the bleachers.

The man on trial looked familiar. Walter vaguely remembered seeing him on the news and taking a special interest in the story. He couldn't place him precisely, not yet.

"Miria, you're supposed to be one of our best guides," said the judge. "What took you so long? We've been waiting for you. I had to postpone judgment on the other souls. The bleachers have filled up."

"I'm sorry, Sir. He gave me a lot of trouble," replied Miria.

The judge furrowed his brows and scanned the branded soul. He was probing the soul with his eyes, attempting to bore into him and analyze the difficulty he might pose. The Truth had released many details on his life, but all of his motivations were not yet clear. Even judges had limited communication with the arbiter of the spiritual realm. Neither guides, judges nor The Truth itself had the power to read minds. Only experience gave insight into the soul and access to information beyond the actions recorded in the physical realm.

The judge relaxed his face after a few moments and leaned back in his chair.

"You're forgiven. I suppose The Truth marked him for a reason."

"Thank you, Sir."

"You're very welcome. This is troubling, though. Surely The Truth would've partially cleansed him to purge his violent tendencies that might make the process difficult. Did he attack you?"

"No, Sir. His mastery of his new spiritual body grew exponentially. He could not attack me due to the cleansing. However, he did attempt to bypass judgment and I was forced to restrain him. It was an extraordinary feat. I've never seen a soul attempt that before."

"That makes sense then. I'm almost as surprised as you, Miria. This is only the third case of attempted bypass I have seen in my long tenure as a judge."

The judge paused for a minute. He rested his chin on his fist in the classic pose and continued staring at the branded soul, deciding how to proceed. The ever-curious Walter took advantage of the lull and questioned Vincent about the proceedings.

"I'm a little confused. How did he try to skip judgment?"

"Strong souls such as him can be difficult to control, while weaker ones such as yourself are easier to handle. Perhaps 'strong' isn't the right word, though."

Vincent took a moment to reformulate his explanation before continuing. Walter prepared himself for further insults and passive aggression. He now knew Vincent well enough to expect such behavior.

"More competent souls can learn to harness their spiritual forms quickly while less competent ones, including David and yourself, will usually not learn anything significant before judgment and aren't capable of struggling against a guide. In other words, a degree of will power and cunning gained in the physical world can be transferred if the soul learns to harness it. Souls that had mediocre intellect and unimpressive will power during their time in the physical realm are never anything to worry about."

"Oh. Good," said Walter a bit sarcastically, trying not to be irked by all the passive aggressive insults.

At this point, Walter knew he was asking for insults and condescension every time he questioned Vincent. He couldn't stop himself, though. He had been curious since his childhood. His curiosity had gotten him into trouble many times in the past and he had learned that acting on it could cost him. Nonetheless, he had not managed to completely control it. If the urge was strong enough, he indulged it and paid the price.

Walter returned his attention to the court as the judge raised his hand to signal the beginning of the trial. An even more powerful wave of hush swept the bleachers. Despite the time the judge took to ponder before the trial, he had not come to any sort of revelation and was still frustrated.

"Alright then. Let's begin. Martin Tomlinson, you have murdered one hundred and fifty-seven people."

Martin did not offer any comment. He wore a blank expression with filmy eyes, his mouth somewhere between smiling and nothing. The judge continued, prompted by the lack of reaction.

"You seem so calm. Aren't you worried about what kind of judgment or punishment The Truth might give you?"

Martin sighed and met the judge's gaze. "I might as well be completely honest since I'm dead so…no, not really. I'm not worried. Once I realized I couldn't get away from this lady," he said as nodded toward Miria, "I decided to just accept all of this, man up and stop running."

The judge wasn't satisfied with this and pressed further. He wanted to at least attempt to give the guides in the bleachers the performance they had anticipated.

"Is there anything else you want to say before I tell you my decision? This could be your last chance to affect the results."

"There isn't much more I want to say," replied Martin. "I did what I need-ed to do. I did what I wanted to do on Earth, so I'll take whatever's coming to me now. I'll admit I was surprised to end up here, though. I'm an Atheist through and through so I definitely thought everything would be done once I was dead. I—"

Martin clearly had more to say, but the judge interrupted him.

"Is that why you killed yourself when you were caught?"

"Yep. I figured I'd cut my losses. After all, there isn't much sense in pros-ecuting a dead guy. Guess that'll backfire if what you guys dish out to me is worse than prison."

"Yes, we can be quite creative here, or rather The Truth can. I don't believe you were finished with your thought, though. Please continue."

"Like I said, it was worth it. Whether it was my main intention or not, you guys can't deny I did some good. Imagine how many more people would've died or gotten raped if I hadn't murdered all those pieces of human garbage. You can argue all day long about them deserving to die or not, but I think it's fair to say the world is better because I took them out. As for arresting them, the whole reason I murdered them was because they'd weaseled out of the law. I always tried to find evidence first and if what you guys said about observing my entire life is true, then you know I'm not lying."

"I'll return the favor and be honest with you, Martin. Your confidence is upsetting. However, I'm not quite sure what to do with you at the moment. You make some good points. Not to say I hadn't considered them already. As you must have inferred by now, our system of justice works differently here. Murdering a man for the purpose of saving others isn't necessarily a sin as far as we are concerned. It can even be worthy of praise and merit in our system. As you said, there is no denying the fact that your killings inadvertently saved the lives of many. Gina Pendleton. She almost certainly would have been bru-tally raped and murdered had you not intervened. This person is only one of hundreds saved by your actions. But notice how I used the word 'inadvertent.' It wasn't your intention to save anyone. It was more of a positive side effect from your need to kill. Am I right?"

"Yeah." Martin replied almost without hesitation. He maintained strict eye contact with the judge. The judge took his hand off his chin and folded his arms before continuing.

"And you're not frightened of the idea of an unknown punishment? It could be anything, Martin. You could rot in prison, you could experience being chopped up without dying. As I said before, we can be very creative here."

The judge saw a chink in Martin's composure for a fraction of a second before he responded. Martin attempted to cover up any signs of fright.

"There's no point in worrying about it before it happens," said Martin. "Whatever's coming to me, I'll take it. There was no way of me knowing what the afterlife was going to be like or if it existed. I was wrong about it not existing and I've admitted that already…so quit trying to scare me and get on with it."

The judge smiled. He was more impressed with Martin's fortitude than he was disappointed in the fact that he couldn't put on a more entertaining show for the audience.

"I'm ashamed to say I'm having trouble with this case. You're Right of Choice will, of course, be revoked. Although the net result was positive, you cannot begin to comprehend the ripple effects of your actions. This isn't the difficult part. The difficult part is the punishment…or whether there should be one. You were meticulous in your killings, Martin. Not a single one of your one hundred and fifty-seven victims were innocent. I'm afraid I'll have to confer with The Truth and ask Miria to hold you in the Secondary Waiting room for now."

Walter felt an air of disappointment in the room, as if the guides wanted to stand up in unison and jeer. Miria watched her back as she opened the door for him. She waited for him to walk ten steps into the waiting room before briefly turning her back so she could close the door quietly. Walter only caught a glimpse of the waiting room. He heard a sample of sound slip through before the door closed. It looked like a prison cell. The sounds of hollers, door buzzers, clanging fences and gates echoed in the abyss. It was The Truth's attempt to give the murderer a taste of the earthly fate he avoided by killing himself before he was captured.

Before the door closed, roughly half of the guides in the bleachers left. They had come without souls and taken advantage of the opportunity to observe the case. Now that is was over, they would return to their observational duties or be tasked with guiding new souls. Walter tilted his head round to get a full view of the courtroom and saw that only ten pairs of guides and souls remained on the western bleachers.

Walter now fully understood the nature of the courtroom. The words "courtroom" and "trial" did not hold the meaning he knew in life. What they represented in the spiritual realm was almost a mockery of their origin. There were no lawyers. There was no defense, prosecution, jury or witnesses. It was a form of entertainment for the spiritual beings, a way for them to soothe the painful boredom of observing and processing souls, the vast majority of which had neither charisma nor notable accomplishments on earth.

All that was necessary for this step in the spiritual processing journey was the judge, the guide, the soul and The Truth. The audience was a gift The Truth had bestowed upon its workers. Between their various observation and processing tasks, it offered a space to relax, mingle and enjoy watching the dissection of the human condition. For some it was a window into their past lives, which carried a warm nostalgia. For others the experience of watching humans triumph and be rewarded or fail and be punished was a voyeuristic pleasure. The worst of the guides were hungry for suffering like spectators at a colosseum, eager to see the most heinous souls punished and humiliated. Hatred was the strongest motivator. Those who hated humans more than anything else in existence reached the height of Schadenfreude when they observed trials.

"Yolanda Smith!" The judge shouted this before the guides finished leaving the courtroom. He wanted to make up for lost time, an intention he made no effort to hide.

Brett led Yolanda to the center of the courtroom. The docility Francis injected into her had worn off. The timing worked because it was no longer necessary. She had finally given up her attempts at suicide and had fallen into a darker depression. Walter watched her with sympathy.

"You've made some trouble since you've gotten here, haven't you Ms. Smith?" He said it like a parent scolding a child, hoping his jovial tone would prop her up for a minute. Yolanda remained silent and let her eyes sink to the floor.

"That's all right. You don't have to say anything. I'll get this over with." The judge cleared his throat before delivering his verdict.

"Yolanda Smith, you will retain your Right of Choice. If you do choose the prescribed fantasy, I can guarantee you will enjoy it. I cannot see what The Truth will prescribe, but I know it will lift your spirits. Perhaps he will allow a servant of faith such as yourself the chance to see the God you imagined all your life. I agree that you deserve such a reward. You have spent your life loving your idea of God and treating others with respect and kindness. You never forced your beliefs upon others and distributed charity to everyone regardless of their own spiritual beliefs. I hope you enjoy what awaits you at the other end of that door."

The judge gestured toward the northeast door marked "Post Judgment." Brett guided Yolanda toward it. Her feet dragged as if they no longer functioned. Brett nearly had to hold her up and sling her over his shoulder as he opened the door. Francis followed quickly behind with David in tow. Now that the door was going to be opened, he took the opportunity to fully process David.

As the door swung open, an almost indescribable mesh of light shone past the threshold and spurted clumsily into the courtroom as if it were alive, deprived of oxygen on the other side and now gasping for breath. There were colors and sights Walter didn't have words for, materials he couldn't categorize. It was a far cry from the cliché image of light at the end of the tunnel. The only part of the void that registered with any human cognition was the part of the atmosphere resembling floating ash and cement. The rest was beyond description.

A tall man in an expensive suit stepped down next. He was the type who might fly back and forth between Wall Street and Hollywood, having contacts in both places. He looked nervous, apprehensive despite the confidence his powerful suit projected. His guide was a woman wearing a modest skirt. She seemed anxious to be done with the trial, itching to get rid of him.

Mere minutes before the trial started, dozens of guides and souls filled the courtroom again

"This case seems simple enough," began the judge. "Frederick LaForet. You were an executive at a studio in California. You raped a number of women over the years. It seems the law never got to you, though. Some of this was because the women you raped didn't want the ordeal to go public and ruin their careers. Other times you bribed them, blackmailed them…or they were too scared. You never suffered any consequences from your actions and instead lost your life from drug use. You're a lucky man, Mr. LaForet, or rather you were until now. Anything to say before I pass judgment?"

LaForet could feel the condemnation of the women in the room. The men surely condemned him as well, but their hatred wasn't strong enough to be palpable. They condemned the act as much as the women but had not experienced the same magnitude of fear during their time alive. They were not nearly as likely to be victims. LaForet felt renewed shame upon realizing the audience regarded the serial killer much more highly.

The judge had seen repeatedly that audiences judged rape far more harshly than the act of intentionally taking a life. There were various reasons for this. Taking a life was not necessarily a sin according to the spiritual processing system. If performed in self-defense, it was acceptable. If enacted to save countless lives and exact justice upon a vile individual, it was sometimes praised, encouraged even.

Even when someone took a life for entirely selfish and malicious reasons, the action did not have to entail as much violation as rape. A gun could not induce the feeling of being violated and humiliated in the worst of ways. Poisoning didn't even require the murderer to be in the same location. Stabbing or beating someone to death were the main methods that carried the same intimacy as rape.

As for as legal punishment on earth, murder was the greater crime and carried more punishment on average. There were, however, many who believed it was worse to force someone to continue living after the trauma and humiliation of a rape. The magnitudes of the punishments varied as well. Murder usually resulted in more jail time. Taking lives could even end in the criminal having his or her own life extinguished in a controversial but legally acceptable manner. Society-endorsed punishments had limitations, though, at least in the physical realm.

"I guess I don't have anything to say. I just-I'm sorry. I'm really sorry. I wish I could take it back," stammered LaForet.

"Why did you do it?" asked the judge.

"I don't know. I just…I don't know."

"You don't know," continued the judge, beginning to sound irritated. "You must have had some reason if you did it so many times. There's no point in lying Mr. LaForet."

The judge snapped his fingers and Mr. LaForet screamed. Walter was startled to see Mr. LaForet clutching his index finger, which had been bent back entirely and broken under the pressure.

"Jesus fucking Christ OK I'll say it!"

"You'll say what? I haven't heard it yet." More fingers broke like kindling. The spiritual beings shuffled in their seats. Some of them craned their necks to get a better view.

"I thought I could get away with it! I knew those bitches would never say anything!" wailed Mr. LaForet. Tears and snot began pouring from him.

"That's much better," said the judge, satisfied he could put on a show for the other spiritual beings. "Now that you've admitted that, let's go ahead and give out the punishment. I think it's fitting you experience the pain and humiliation you inflicted on your victims. The Truth will have the final say, but I'm confident your punishment will be somewhat along those lines. That is all."

The judge motioned for the guide to take Mr. LaForet to the post-judgment door.

"Wait! Wait, what does he mean by that? What's gonna happen to me?" cried Mr. LaForet as he looked to his guide in desperation.

The guide lowered her head and ignored him. He began to resist and she quickly subdued him by using her fingers to inject him the way Francis had done earlier. She then tossed him into the void behind the doorway similar to how a bartender might throw out a belligerent drunk. Some of the people in the stands clapped. Applause from scattered members of the audience crescendoed and then fell. The failed unanimity of enthusiasm for such a punishment created an awkwardness that made many people in the bleachers uncomfortable, especially those who had clapped.

"Wait so is that guy going to get raped?" asked Walter, turning to Vincent in hopes of disproving his assumption.

"He will experience the pain and humiliation he inflicted upon his victims. It most likely means he will experience being raped in one manner or another," Vincent responded coldly.

"Is that really necessary?"

"The Truth is not concerned with what is necessary, only what is just."

"I see. It seems kind of messed up is all. I don't know if 'just' is the right word."

"It is justice. *Our* justice. Perhaps you are too small-minded to understand."

"I think I'm smart enough to understand that two wrongs don't always make a right. Raping him isn't going to do anything for the women he raped."

"You're absolutely right. It won't do anything for the women he raped. They will have to live the rest of their lives with the trauma as best they can. It is too late for them to receive justice now that Mr. LaForet is dead. That isn't the point, though. The punishments here serve not as justice for the victims but rather as a method of ensuring criminals pay for their sins in the afterlife if they have not paid while alive. It is justice for the sake of justice. I have my grievances with The Truth and certain aspects of our spiritual processing system, but I must praise this element of it. The Truth takes full advantage of its unlimited resources in the ability to make people experience situations as if they were still in the physical realm. Such punishments and rewards cannot be administered in a human justice system."

Vincent paused for a moment before continuing. He looked at Walter and their eyes met.

"Before you respond, let me ask you something Walter. Do you think it would be just for someone like Mr. LaForet to be spared a punishment in the afterlife?"

Walter was pleasantly surprised to see Vincent beginning to engage him in a real discussion rather than going on with his usual condescending lectures. He wasn't sure of the answer, though. He hadn't finished formulating his thoughts, but he decided to respond before losing the opportunity.

"I agree he should be punished and lose his Right of Choice. It's just really unsettling to know that a man is being put through a so-called *system* so he can experienced being raped. And then what happens? That's it right? He's gonna get raped and then become nothing. He doesn't get a chance to make things right? He doesn't get a chance to make up for what he did?"

"I understand your points. I suppose there isn't a correct answer to the question of what to do with sinful souls. My theory, however, is that The Truth has limited power and must reserve more extended fantasies and second lives for souls who have done a multitude of good deeds on Earth. Even if my theory were completely wrong, though, I think your approach is too compassionate. I don't think this aspect of the current system needs any modification."

Walter decided to make a crude segue. He realized his discussion with Vincent wouldn't progress any further. Still, he wanted to know more about The Truth by taking advantage of Vincent's talkative mood and the current lull in exciting trials.

"Speaking of compassion, does this Truth thing have any of it? Based on what I've seen in the trials so far, it seems like a sort of computer system that assigns rewards and punishments based on the person and the things they did."

"The Truth can be mysterious even to us guides. Even the judges who have spoken with it cannot verify whether it has emotions or understanding of a human experience beyond observation."

"What do you think about it? You mentioned 'grievances' before."

"I am not required to discuss such matters. Besides, the next trial is starting, so we should hold our discussion."

"I have a feeling you're never gonna tell me."

"If you are judged well and if we have time after the trial, I will answer any non-required questions you have to the best of my ability. What you know about me and The Truth will not matter after the trial anyway."

Walter didn't feel confident that Vincent would completely indulge his curiosity. Although Vincent had been honest so far, Walter perceived his offer as more of a placation than a promise.

Most of the spiritual beings not currently attending to a soul exited the room. They knew the next few cases weren't particularly interesting. They were all people who had lived boring lives nearly void of sin or notable accomplishment. The judge waved most of them through without even having a "trial."

"Let's see… our next case is Stacy Brigham. She's led an excellent life with little sin and plenty of service for others. Oh, there is one blemish, though. Posthumous baptisms as part of the Mormon faith…including some Jews from the Holocaust. That's a shame. This would've been an easy decision otherwise."

"What do you think of her, Isaac? Would I be too harsh to take away her Right of Choice over this matter?"

"She's a wonderful woman, your honor. She's done nothing wrong in any other regard. She's been charitable and kind to others all her life. I think the posthumous baptisms had more to do with her husband's influence. I don't think Mrs. Brigham had any desire to disrespect the dead."

"True, but is that a valid excuse? People still have their own will even when influenced by others."

Her guide, Isaac, solemnly nodded his head in agreement, disappointed that his input wasn't enough to completely sway the judge.

"Let me ask you something then Mrs. Brigham," continued the judge. "What did you think you were accomplishing when you performed these baptisms?"

She hesitated for a moment. Nonetheless, she had learned from Mr. LaForet's example and decided to be immediately honest.

"I never really thought they did anything. A lot of things in that religion seemed like nonsense to me, but I went along with it because I knew how much it meant to my husband."

"Well then, it gives me great pleasure to tell you that your posthumous baptisms had no effect. I'm afraid the version of God your husband believed in doesn't exist and that Joseph Smith was merely a conman. The act, however, is disrespectful even if it has no consequences. Wouldn't you agree?"

"I'm not sure I understand. How is it disrespectful?"

Isaac shook his head and attempted to signal to her that she should agree with the judge without question. The judge caught this and glared at him. Like The Truth, judges could communicate to spiritual beings without human souls being able to hear. They could, however, only do so within a certain proximity. On the other hand, The Truth could communicate limitlessly with souls and spiritual beings.

"Don't help her, Isaac," hissed the judge, his words rattling around in only Isaac's mind. "She needs to demonstrate some remorse before I can be completely sure she is worthy of being rewarded in the afterlife. She needs to realize her actions were wrong despite the harmless intentions. Otherwise, the sin might affect her post-judgment."

Isaac lowered his head and turned away from Mrs. Brigham. The abrupt pause confused Mrs. Brigham because she couldn't hear any of the conversation. The judge put his eyes back on Mrs. Brigham and continued.

"Let me explain it to you this way, Mrs. Brigham. I believe no one should compromise the identity of the dead. Imagine if you passed away and then a Jewish person declared you as a Jew in both life and death. This would be inaccurate wouldn't it?"

"Yes."

"Indeed, it would. Would this Jewish person really have any right to modify your identity after you died? Assuming the baptism did have an effect, wouldn't it be disrespectful to make that choice on your behalf even if they believed it granted you salvation in heaven? Wouldn't it rudely imply that Judaism is superior to what you believed in?"

"I see your point, your honor. I wouldn't like that." Mrs. Brigham played with her hair a little in contemplation before continuing. It had been obscuring her vision.

"Maybe there were times when I thought it was wrong. I didn't want to let my family down, though. I didn't want to be the stick in the mud. Still, I'm sorry. It was wrong."

"You are forgiven, my dear. I would not have taken away your Right of Choice even if you did not repent. It is such a minor sin with no real impact. I am not so cruel despite what some people around here might think," said the judge, glancing at Isaac. "I merely wanted to see how you felt about it because your feelings might affect what The Truth prescribes for you in post-judgment. You're a kind woman and I'm sure you'll be granted a wonderful fantasy if you make that choice."

"Thank you, your honor."

Isaac put his hand on Mrs. Brigham's shoulder and guided her toward the post-judgment door. Walter moved to the edge of his seat in anticipation of the door opening and showing a glimpse of the void beyond.

The next soul walked toward the podium with an ambiguous aura, exuding something between confidence and delusion. Part of this was because he had arrived after Mr. LaForet's trial was over.

His skin was oddly orange. He had thin blond hair that also looked suspicious. It stood up high, yet it seemed empty, like a gentle breeze could blow it away. He wore a black suit with an almost comically long red tie. As he approached the podium, each step made the end of it flop awkwardly around his crotch.

"Let's see…Mr. Spieler, you ran a business for many years before starting a career in politics. Due to your reckless actions, people lost their homes and livelihoods. You also scammed people with numerous fraudulent businesses. The numbers of lies you have told is unprecedented, even for someone in both politics and business. Then there are the sexual assaults and harassments, the most heinous crimes, yet the ones you faced the least amount of consequences for on Earth. Do you have anything to say before I tell you your fate?"

"I don't think I deserve a punishment. I was a great politician and businessman, the best. Everybody loved me. Everything I did was within the law. The sex stuff is bogus. It's a bunch of conspiracy theories from all the fake news people out to get me."

As he spoke he moved his arms around in circles. These gestures brought attention to how small his hands were in comparison to the bulky suit he used to hide his obesity.

"You disgust me," replied the judge. "Even after your guide told you he witnessed everything in your life, you still insist on lying about…"

"Excuse me!" interrupted Spieler.

"Don't you dare interrupt me!" barked the judge. The moment the judge raised his voice, Spieler went silent. Spieler's mouth was still moving, but no sound could escape it.

The judge was only beginning to flex his power. His eyes widened and he stood up. His hands were still relaxed, though. Unlike the guides, he didn't need to use hand gestures to manipulate souls. Spieler suddenly started gasping for air.

"You may have had power on Earth, but you are nothing here," said the judge. "There is no money to protect you from our punishments. You have no lawyers, followers, employees or surrogates."

Now Spieler was on the floor, nearly unconscious. The air in the courtroom shifted. An invisible pressure was pushing it upward. People in the bleachers could still breathe, but their air had become thinner.

After a few moments, the air returned to normal and Spieler regained consciousness. The judge was far from finished, though. Spieler's clothes suddenly flew off. Despite his gut covering most of his penis and drooping testicles, he instinctively covered his crotch. Then he frantically looked around, unable to completely grasp what was happening. His mouth was flapping furiously, but he still couldn't generate sound. He didn't know this, though. To him it appeared as if everyone around him had become deaf. Because of the embarrassment and stress, it was difficult for him to think outside himself, even more so than usual.

The judge manipulated the invisible forces of the spiritual realm and used them to hoist Spieler by his wrists. The audience gasped as he rose into the air and wriggled like a fish on a pole. The shock made his face so bright with blemishes that it almost matched his hair.

Then the judge walked close to Spieler. His gate was slow, deliberately cinematic. He raised his hand and perched it atop an invisible target the way a bird would use its talons to capture prey. He then whipped his hand backward, causing a ripping sound to echo through the court. Exclamations filled with expletives erupted from the audience. A few people screamed.

Spieler's hair drifted slowly to the floor. Pieces of skin were attached to the ends of it. For a seemingly thick piece of hair, it was surprisingly light. The middle of his scalp was bald, but there were red lines on the sides where hair had once sprouted. An increasing amount of blood trickled down his body and dripped onto the floor along with a sprinkling of tears.

"OK, Mr. Spieler," announced the judge. "I'll allow you some closing remarks before I tell you your sentence."

For a few seconds everyone in the courtroom could hear Spieler's earsplitting screams. The voice was foreign. The pain and humiliation had removed its snide undertones. The crowd cringed. Then Spieler went silent again.

"If that's all, I'll go ahead with the punishment I will propose to The Truth," continued the judge. "You will spend ten years living as a disfigured homeless man while retaining memories of your former life. During the first year five years, you will not have the ability to speak. For the last five years, you will be able to speak, but only if you tell the truth. If you attempt to lie, your words will be silent. You will also not be able to kill yourself to end the simulation prematurely. Men will assault, rape and sexually harass you at random intervals. That is all."

The door to post-judgment opened and Spieler went sliding along the floor and through the threshold. It slammed shut behind him. As the void washed over him and began to cleanse him, he felt unexpected relief. There was only nothingness. There was no audience to perform for. Being alone felt acceptable for the first time. The swirling pieces of ash began perforating his soul, causing his insecurities to bleed out. The burden was gone.

The blood stains on the floor shrank and disappeared one by one. It was as if some internal sun had rapidly evaporated them before they could soak into the floor.

"Listen, everyone," shouted the judge. "In the spiritual realm, your sins and good deeds are all that matter. We don't care about how much privilege or wealth you had on Earth. Unless you are craving an extra punishment, do not waste my time with lies. People like Mr. Spieler are not safe. They will face consequences for their sins."

A few people in the crowd applauded. Then it spread like a virus until nearly half the people in the bleachers were bringing their hands together. Walter was surprised at himself as he realized how tempted he was to join his fellow souls, how satisfied he was with the prospect of the punishment. The rape aspect of the punishment disturbed him, but he approved of the rest of it. He felt like a hypocrite. Why was he appraising most of this punishment as being so righteous while the one for Mr. LaForet seemed extreme?

It might have been because Walter knew who Mr. Spieler was. He had heard about the sexual assault allegations, the lies, the fraudulent businesses and his ambition of becoming president. It was a relief to see he had died before rising in the polls. Walter could only imagine the horrors of someone like Spieler becoming the most powerful person in the world.

Whenever thought-provoking events like this confronted Walter, he retreated into his mind so he could fully evaluate the situation and its implications. He went into a sort of trance where his entire being became temporarily numb to his surroundings. It formed a bubble around him that muted the crowd. Only noises pertinent to him and Vincent would break through. In this mental realm, Walter could perform a sort of Socratic method where his mind created two characters with two distinct voices: the one who questions and the one who attempts to answer, sometimes using more questions.

Time felt slower when he did this. There were instances in his childhood when he would daydream, only intending to do so for a minute, and then finish to find half an hour had passed by and that he had no idea what had happened during this period. He wished he could bring the universe to a halt, that there was some sort of time chamber he could retreat to and emerge from once he had organized his thoughts.

The first epic daydream occurred as a teenager when his mother brought him along during her checkup at a free clinic. Because the wait was terribly long, Walter passed the time by daydreaming. He looked at the fish tank against the wall. His mind left the room as he thought about how the fish had been acquired and what motivation there was to have a fish in the waiting room. Why had it become such a standard? What value was there? Was the amount of money needed for the maintenance worth the aesthetic value? Why was it often a fish when there were other small animals that could provide more entertainment for a reduced price?

When Walter had finished considering the possible answers to this series of questions, he awoke to find his surroundings were different. Most of the people in the waiting room had left, replaced by new faces. His mother was now second in line. More than an hour had gone by in a time that, to him, only felt like minutes. He came to believe that only detachment from the majority of one's surrounding stimuli could unlock latent ability for reasoning, imagination and analysis. Walter was no seasoned philosopher, though. He was simply an experienced daydreamer.

Walter began by reappraising the value of the rewards the spiritual processing system offered vs. rewards in the physical realm. The experiences and assurances were key. In the physical realm, luck was an enormous factor in determining whether people received rewards for hard work and good deeds. Hard work didn't guarantee success, kindness toward others didn't guarantee any sort of reciprocation, and other kinds of rewards did not necessarily come in the form people desired. The actions themselves could also act as a reward if the person enjoyed them.

The rewards in the afterlife accounted for these facts. People who performed good deeds could be rewarded if they died before experiencing the fruits of their labor or did not receive significant compensation. The elements the physical realm could not provide for them became accessible if they were worthy. Cripples could walk, the blind could see and those who had lost their loved ones could reunite, assuming they had performed enough positive actions to be deserving of such rewards. The rewards also considered those who had suffered from resisting desires they were cursed with and unable to act upon without condemnation from society. Pedophiles who never molested children, who performed deeds beneficial to society in spite of their travails, could experience a world where their actions were perfectly legal. Although the thought disturbed Walter, he had no idealistic opposition to it. He believed Vincent's assertion that the fantasy rewards were harmless. Overall, he thought the reward aspect of the system was wonderful.

The vast majority of Walter's criticisms of the spiritual system concerned the punishments. He mused upon the nature of punishment in the physical realm and realized there were generally two forms of legal punishment people around the world agreed were reasonable: loss of money in the form of fines, tickets, and lawsuits, and time spent in prison. The death penalty was another option but was too controversial in many countries.

As Vincent implied earlier, these punishments existed and dominated, in part, because of limitations in the physical world. There were some ludicrous sentences judges could give, but these were relatively rare. People still generally could not tailor punishments to the individual and subject them to ironic situations based on their crimes. Rapists could not experience being raped. Even if the technology had been developed, there would be a lot of moral resistance to it. The spiritual realm made new possibilities for punishments that, despite opposition from more considerate and merciful people such as Walter, had value and support from most of the souls and guides who passed through the system.

Walter fell deeper into his rumination when this interesting question arose: What would happen in the physical realm if technology existed that could dole out rewards and punishments in the way The Truth did? Would people accept this technology as a substitute for prison sentences or at least an alternative to it? If so, how long would this acceptance take?

Walter shook his head. These questions could go on for a while. He decided to restore focus by continuing with the other kind of punishment, the one that was harder to quantify and more dependent on luck: negative consequences from a legal sin. If a business' CEO expressed homophobic views, they might lose a number of customers, which one could perceive as a sort of punishment for bigotry and ignorance. If a husband repeatedly committed adultery, he would not be breaking the law. His spouse, however, could leave him, divorce him or murder him for revenge. Again, it came down to luck.

The word "luck" brought Walter to the prospect of his own judgment. The philosophical wanderer chided himself immediately for not starting his queries with his trial after realizing that his feelings toward the system might be inconsequential. It was naïve of him to believe he could make large-scale changes on his own. The Truth controlled everything. His criticisms also did not reflect any sort of consensus among souls or spiritual beings.

Walter decided to finish his queries by once again evaluating his chances for a successful judgment. He was confident he would not receive an extreme punishment. The only major sin he committed was the assault on his mother's boyfriend. Keeping his Right of Choice seemed likely but not certain.

Then there was the question of what would happen if he did keep his Right of Choice. Vincent had stated several times that Walter had not accomplished anything noteworthy. He had not performed a significant number of good deeds, nor were these deeds impressive. Was he worthy of enjoying a prescribed fantasy? If so, did he deserve a prescribed fantasy with his wife in it, which was the only kind of reward he wanted? Once again, it was all luck. It was all subjective. There could be no guarantee or certainty.

"Walter Klein," shouted the judge.

Walter nearly jumped out of his seat as this cue perforated his bubble. The daydreamer realized two trials had gone by during his extended ponderings. The mental absence reminded him of all the instances when he had mourned the events that blurred by him during his introspection, worried he was wasting precious moments. Fear did not envelop him, though. For the first time in his existence, he praised himself for burrowing deep into his psyche, believing the brief journey would grant him the answer to the choice he would make if judged well. He was ready, confident and resolute.

Three

As Walter and Vincent rose, the audience turned their heads in a nearly synchronized wave of motion. The pair proceeded down the stairs and toward the center of the courtroom. Vincent turned to Walter and spoke softly, not quite a whisper but not loud enough for the judge to hear.

"You most likely considered this already, but please don't lie to the judge. It wouldn't be wise. Address him respectfully, tell the entire truth and don't mind the audience."

"Got it."

Walter had been forming his thoughts during the less interesting trials. He had rehearsed anything he might have to say regarding the incident with his mother's meal ticket. He also picked his choice in the event he was judged well. He only thought about what he would do if he retained his Right of Choice because his desires wouldn't matter if he lost it.

"The Truth has advised me to pay special attention to you, Walter," said the judge. "I fail to understand why, though. Your life doesn't seem remarkable to me. As for your troublesome curiosity, it's almost common in my experience, nothing special really. The Truth is excellent at predicting the future, though, so perhaps it is something yet to happen that makes you a Special Focus soul. On second thought, there is little that could happen between now and when you are processed. I can't imagine what significant event might occur. Hmmm…"

The judge paused and tapped on his podium for a few seconds before looking at Vincent.

"So Vincent, what do you think of him? Any theories as to why The Truth would demand a Special Focus be put on him?"

"Mr. Klein can be insolent at times, but he is a good man." Walter beamed for a moment, reveling in the closest thing to a compliment Vincent had given him.

"Words like special or extraordinary do not describe him, though. I think 'mediocre' is the best fit," continued Vincent. "I have thought hard about it but cannot think of any reason why The Truth would demand extra attention be given to him."

Vincent decided to bludgeon away the fleeting feeling of positivity Walter might experience from his initial complement. Walter expected a strike of negativity after such rare praise and was already proficient at brushing off such insults.

The judge chuckled in reaction to Vincent and addressed the guide as if he were an old friend.

"There's no need to be so harsh. This makes me happy, though. I'm glad to see you haven't changed a bit." The judge was prompting a response from Vincent, hoping for a friendly conversation before the proceedings. Vincent wasn't interested. He wore a blank expression, indicating he had nothing more to say. It became clear to the room that the air of warmth between Vincent and the judge was one-sided. The judge gave up on waiting for Vincent. He cleared his throat in an attempt to hide his disappointment. Then he placed his frustration onto Walter with a glare and began the trial.

"Vincent, do you have anything to say before I pass judgment?"

"No. Nothing more."

Part 4

One

Walter's mother, Hilda, spent her early childhood privileged and un-loved. She was the daughter of a wealthy businessman. For a while, all she knew about her father and mother was they made enough money for them to have a big house and hire a maid. She didn't fully understand what the business was. The closest thing to an answer her father had given was that they "were in the restaurant business." Even when her parents were in the house, they rarely interacted with her, usually too tired or uninterested.

They were only warm and affectionate toward her at church. They smiled and held her hand so they could paint the picture of a perfect family for the public. Once they got back in the car, the temperature dropped back to the icy normal.

While she was playing in their expansive living room one day, two intimi-dating men in suits arrived. The maid nervously opened the door for them.

"Is this the residence of Charles and Maria Ellingwood?" said the taller man.

"Y-Yes," stammered the maid.

"We have a warrant to search the premises. Please step aside." He handed her a smooth piece of paper, neatly folded and stamped, as he pushed the door completely open and entered the mansion.

"Look at all this fancy shit," said the shorter man in a suit as he surveyed the foyer and made his way to the living room. He slapped his fingers down forcefully on the mahogany cabinets along the sides of the wall. While exhal-ing loudly, he enjoyed the texture and rubbed the rest of the material, almost petting it. "Just this little entrance is probably worth more than my apartment. How much do you think the government will make from it?"

"Millions at least. We don't know until the paperwork comes through and we get permission to seize all of it."

"Do you think any of the whores they kidnapped will get a cut of it as compensation?"

"Maybe. I hope so."

"Fucking rich pricks! I hope they get…"

"Hold it!" interrupted the tall man as he noticed Hilda playing in the living room. The short man cursed his loose tongue, hoping the child hadn't been paying attention. Hilda eyed them apprehensively as they neared her. Her favorite teddy bear lay in her arms. Her father had brought strange men over before, but this time felt different.

"You must be Hilda," said the tall man, kneeling down so his towering presence might not frighten her as much. "I'm sorry we had to come barging in like this. I'm Howard. This is my partner, Jaime."

Howard extended his hand slowly. He gripped the entirety of Hilda's wrist with only a few fingers and moved it up and down slowly, hardly a shake. Jaime smiled and nodded as Hilda gazed up at him. He stayed silent, still guilty about swearing in the child's presence.

"We need you to come with us to the police station if that's all right," continued Howard.

"What's going on? Where's my mom and dad?"

Howard took a deep breath before he continued. He scratched his forehead as he calculated a way to answer her question without being hurtful.

"You see, Hilda, my partner and I look for people who make big mistakes in their lives. When we find them, we have to take them away so they don't make more mistakes and hurt more people."

"Who'd they hurt?"

"A lot of people. You'll understand when you're older."

"Where are they?"

"They're away right now."

Hilda couldn't decide how to feel. Becoming sad because of someone's absence meant having an attachment to begin with. Since she could remember being alive, there was no love in her family. Her parents' disappearance was more confusing than heartbreaking.

"We need you to come down to the police station with us," continued Howard. "Your Aunt Gloria and Uncle Mario are waiting there. You're going to be living with them for a while."

Gloria was her mother's sister. She had also emigrated from Mexico but had, unlike her sister, married for love instead of wealth. She worked as a chef for a local bakery and restaurant. She met her husband, Mario, when he was hired as a contractor to extend the restaurant. Once Gloria's sister married her husband, she ignored Gloria. She didn't want to be associated with her former life of poverty and struggling.

Gloria was bitter about this and considered sending Hilda to an orphanage as a sort of revenge. She purged this evil thought, however, and decided adopting Hilda permanently was the right decision. Past grudges couldn't dilute her blood enough to forget Hilda was a family member. Gloria also understood both her sister and brother-in-law might not be coming out of jail any time soon.

Despite hesitations and assumptions Gloria had about Hilda, they grew to love each other quickly. Most of their bond came from teaching one another. Hilda helped Mario and Gloria improve their English because they had not learned it formally. In turn, Gloria and Mario ensured Hilda mastered both English and Spanish.

The foster parents adopted her. She adopted their values and personality traits as if it were thicker in her blood than that of her biological parents. She never called them "Mom" or "Dad" but still saw them as parents because they were the first people to give her love and attention. The desire to visit her actual parents did not arise. Her curiosity about what they had done festered, though. After a few years of living with Gloria and Mario she could no longer ignore it.

"Auntie, can I ask you something?"

"What is it?" replied Gloria as she was chopping up plantains, readying them to be cooked and served for dinner later. The up and down motion of the knife made ripples in her body, causing the rolls of fat around her waist to dance in a steady rhythm.

"What did my mom and dad do? Why did they go to jail?"

The question startled her. She almost fumbled her knife.

"Why do you want to know that now? You haven't said a thing about it since you moved in."

"I'm old enough! I want to know!" Hilda had recently turned fourteen, forcing the issue of age to the front of her mind.

"Calm down," said Gloria.

"I'm sorry, Auntie. I'm just tired of people lying to me or not telling me anything. I want to know."

Gloria walked over to the kitchen table and gestured toward the other side, inviting Hilda to take a seat. Her hesitations reminded Gloria of how Howard behaved when they met. The consideration for her innocence as a minor was still annoying rather than appreciated.

"There isn't a nice way for me to say this to you." Gloria paused again before continuing. "They owned slaves."

This bewildered Hilda. As far as she understood, slavery was extinct.

"I thought slavery ended after the Civil War. That's what my textbook says."

Gloria laughed a bit at her niece's naivety but then stopped herself, worrying she might appear insensitive.

"You can't believe everything you read in books. There are still slaves. It just isn't in the open the way it used to be."

"I don't really get it."

Gloria stood up and opened a drawer on a small stand next to the sink. She had to unlock this one with a key. Inside it was a pile of old newspapers. Gloria ruffled through them for a few moments before pulling out a few Union Tribune papers dated several years ago. She set them down on the table and gave Hilda a solemn look.

"If you want to know everything, you can read these. I'm warning you, though. You can't pretend you didn't read it. You can't blame me if it makes you cry."

"I won't cry," yelled Hilda defiantly. Gloria threw up her hands in a mock surrender and quietly walked out of the room.

Later that night Hilda began looking through the newspapers. As she scanned the articles, a few lines stood out.

"Wealthy Couple Arrested for Sex Trafficking Operation"

"...sex trafficking scandal rocked La Jolla..."

"Each restaurant had back rooms and basements where waitresses and workers would perform sexual favors"

"Many of the prostitutes and servers had been sold or bonded into debt and then illegally immigrated"

"Some were brutally beaten for insubordination"

There were a few images strewn throughout the pages. The first displayed the Marquee of the restaurant chain, "Oaxaca Grill." Hilda cringed as she thought of all the times her parents had taken her there, how all the meals were free for some reason. The next photo showed one of the notorious basement rooms. It was about the same size as Hilda's current room. Each wall, with the exception of the one with the door, had a three-level bunk. "A minimum of nine people slept in this room," according to the caption below. The picture alone portrayed how filthy and dank those quarters were, the unspeakable transgressions that might've transpired there.

Hilda became nauseous as she fully digested the articles. She finally understood why her parents were so cold and emotionless. Only monsters devoid of empathy could knowingly subject dozens of people to modern slavery, forcing them into conditions where offering their bodies was the only method of survival, where escape meant deportation, arrest or death. Everything Hilda had seen was fake, a farce designed to wrap the hideous truth in a layer of aesthetic beauty. The affection in the church was only an attempt to cast off suspicion. The secrets, meetings with shady characters and the men in suits reached a painful clarity. Tears dripped off her cheeks and lips and onto the pages. They wetted and smeared the ink on some of the most revealing sentences. It was as if the tears themselves could not bear to look any longer. The salty water entered her mouth and tickled her throat, causing her to sputter more on the pages.

Mario knocked gently on the door. Hilda tried to wipe away evidence of her outburst before he stepped into the room.

"Are you OK?"

"I wasn't crying. I just have a cough."

Mario chuckled. "It's OK to cry, Hilda. Your Auntie is tough about stuff like that, but don't worry. I've seen her cry before."

"Really?"

"Yes. Shhh. It'll be our secret," he said coyly, putting his finger to his lips and smiling.

Hilda giggled. Mario noticed the newspaper she was hiding behind her back now that she had let her guard down. He took them from her gently. Then the two embraced. Hilda smiled and nestled her head into his chest as he held her. She cherished the sensation of his fingers, calloused and peppery from construction work, bristling the back of her neck. His touch, however uncomfortable it could be at times, was genuine. The only time she felt her parents' skin upon her own was at church. Even then the contact was meaningless. Warm hands made of mud were vastly superior to cold hands molded from ivory.

"It's not your fault," he whispered.

———•———

Although Mario's words comforted her, Hilda began changing significantly after that day. For her, it was no longer enough for the truth to exist. It had to be told. Every inch, detail and angle of it had to be divulged so there would be no lingering questions, no delusions, no pretenses. She believed the reality of a situation should mirror its aesthetics and vice versa. Language should be raw and irreverent so it could convey the height of both the hideousness and beauty of truth. Everything had to be direct. She developed a way of communicating that was unapologetic, honest, unfiltered and rude at times. She absorbed the blunt ways of her new guardians, especially her aunt, and then embellished upon them.

The combination of her name, behavior and appearance confused her peers as she developed into a young woman. Hilda wasn't the kind of name most people associated with an attractive woman. People imagined girls named Hilda coming out of the womb as either short old women with hunched backs or muscular giants with little feminine grace. She was beautiful, with the mannerisms of a "barrio girl" as her classmates called her. Because she was ashamed of her background, Hilda accepted her image as a poor, lower-class girl. She had trouble making friends in high school, that is until she met Eugene.

She bumped into him while he was waiting in line for his school lunch. She had already picked hers up, so the collision caused her to spill the food all over Eugene.

"Sorry," said Eugene.

"What do you mean, 'Sorry?' I bumped into you and now my shitty mashed potatoes are all over you. Why are you apologizing?"

"Oh, I know. I meant I'm sorry you'll have to buy a new lunch. I can pay for it if you want."

"Are you serious?"

"Yeah. Of course I am."

Hilda was stunned for a second. She didn't know whether to be grateful or disgusted by his spinelessness. She chose the latter after a few more seconds.

"You seriously need to grow some balls. Just because I'm a girl doesn't mean it's OK for me to knock over your food," she hissed as she walked away.

After that, Hilda couldn't stop thinking about Eugene. It perplexed her. She used to imagine being interested in a confident guy, maybe a typical bad boy. Still, she decided she had to deal with her feelings for him in the direct manner she believed was honorable.

"So I guess I like you or something," said Hilda abruptly as she sat down next to Eugene during the school lunch break.

"What?" said Eugene, a little surprised.

"I don't get why," continued Hilda. "You're not that tall. I might even be a little taller than you. You don't seem real smart or strong either. Maybe something's wrong with my brain."

"Well, I am pretty handsome," said Eugene in mock seriousness, raising his eyebrows up and down in order to tease Hilda.

"No you're not," she retorted.

"Yes I am."

"Who says that? I bet no one has ever said you're handsome."

"My Grandma says I am. But then again she's my Grandma so she has to say things like that. Even if she meant it, her vision is pretty bad so maybe it's not really a compliment." Eugene would later pass down his occasional habit of thinking aloud.

Hilda laughed. His awkwardness and sincerity had charm.

The pair had lunch every day after that and began dating shortly after. She realized Eugene shared her values but had a completely different way of expressing them. They learned surprising facts about one another as well. Beneath Hilda's seemingly mean spirit and sharp tongue lay deep empathy and consideration for others. In turn, Hilda saw that Eugene was capable of being assertive and serious when the situation demanded it. His passive nature did not carry the weaknesses Hilda initially assumed. The pair fell deeply in love. They decided to get married and live together shortly after graduating high school.

As they climbed the steps to their studio apartment with boxes in hand, Gloria and Mario followed behind with lighter boxes.

"I still think this is crazy. You kids have lost it," grumbled Gloria as she set her box down carelessly on the floor, forgetting about whether or not the contents were fragile.

"Tell us how you really feel, Auntie," teased Hilda as she set her own box on the empty mattress.

"Why don't you live with us until you make more money?" said Gloria.

"We wouldn't want to impose, Mrs. Rodriguez," interjected Eugene as he set down some cheap folding chairs.

"You can call her Gloria now, babe. We're married."

"No he can't! I wasn't talking to him anyway!" shouted Gloria, who had now begun speaking in Spanish so she could exclude Eugene from the conversation. "This whole thing is crazy. You're too young. Finish school first!"

"Didn't you and Uncle get married right out of high school? You didn't go to college either," retorted Hilda, now speaking in Spanish as well.

"This isn't about me. You should do what I say, not what I've done before."

"Mrs. Rodriguez," began Eugene nervously, as it was the first time he was testing out his Spanish on someone other than Hilda. "I don't think us being married will stop her from going to school if she wants to. We've been looking into affordable programs. I understand why you're upset, though."

"He can speak Spanish?" hissed Gloria.

"I've been teaching him," said Hilda, grinning deliberately. "You'll have to watch what you say from now on."

Gloria glared at Eugene. He blushed. Meanwhile Mario spectated and unsuccessfully tried to contain his laughter so his wife would not hear.

"What's so funny? I'm being serious here," said Gloria.

"Nothing, mi amor. I think maybe we should leave the lovebirds alone. All the boxes are in now."

After a bit more quarreling, Gloria, Mario, and Hilda kissed each other goodbye. Mario shook Eugene's hand and gave him a slightly embarrassed expression as if to say, "Sorry about my wife. For the record, I think you're all right." Eugene smiled at both of them as they left and quietly closed the door.

"Sorry about my Auntie," said Hilda. "She'll warm up to you eventually. She's just freaking out because I'm not following her whole, 'no boys until after school' dogma."

"I know. Don't worry about it." Eugene put his arm around her and glanced at her stomach. "When are we going to tell them about the baby?"

"Soon," replied Hilda. "I didn't want to do it today. One bombshell at a time, you know. I feel like she would have a heart attack if she had to deal with both in one day."

"Good point."

The newlyweds were silent for a minute as they surveyed the apartment and all the unopened boxes.

"Are you sure there will be room for the baby?" said Hilda.

"For a baby, yes. We'll have more money and a bigger place by the time he gets bigger. By the way, I thought of a name."

"Oh. What is it?"

"Walter. It was my buddy's name, the guy who passed away."

"Hmmm…it's pretty white-sounding for a mixed baby, but I guess I like it."

Hilda and Eugene only made enough money to survive and eat healthily. They were happy, though. Both of them took jobs at the zoo so they could be together. People continued pressuring them to start careers or go to college, but neither had the money for a good school nor did they know what they wanted to do with their careers. Hilda devoted some of her time to activism against human trafficking. It was hard, however, to find an activism career with any money. They also had to take care of Walter. There wasn't time for anything other than work.

Eugene started his career by chance. He went to shooting ranges and hunting with a rifle during his free time. He was excellent. He rarely missed and managed to hit the most difficult targets. An ex-military sniper spotted him at the range and referred him to a training program for sharpshooters. Eugene accepted and planned to use the GI Bill to go to college, get a better paying career and ultimately a better future once he was done with his service.

Eugene had hesitations about sniping due to his compassion. He talked about it with Hilda before deciding to join the program.

"It'll be like shooting pumpkins. 'Pretend they're pumpkins' is what I meant to say." Hilda wasn't great at comforting people, but she tried her best with Eugene.

"Pumpkins don't have families waiting for them," said Eugene.

"These are bad people, Gene. You don't have to feel sorry for them."

"You're right. Maybe I'm being selfish. This isn't only about me after all."

Eugene petted Walter's head. His son's hair had become so thick already and he had begun speaking and walking. Eugene had trouble processing how quickly the years had gone by since Walter was born and how he had managed to complete his military training.

"You might not have to shoot anyone if you're lucky" added Hilda.

"That's true."

Eugene never *did* get a chance to snipe anyone. He was one of the American coalition members taken by a scud missile during Operation Desert Storm.

Two

Hilda was distraught. She wore the traditional black, left Walter in Gloria and Mario's care for two weeks and took time off from work until she was through the worst of the grieving process. She wondered how she would manage to raise Walter on her own. She wondered how growing up without a father might affect him.

Despite his father's absence, Walter grew up to be the product one would expect from Hilda and Eugene. He had his father's awkward charms and compassion along with his mother's feistiness and curiosity. Hilda simultaneously loved and resented these traits Walter had inherited. It made her feel as if a part of Eugene had remained, that she had not lost him completely. On the other hand, it reminded her he was gone and she would most likely not find another man like him.

It was hard being a yang and raising Walter now that her yin was gone.

Eugene taught her that self-censorship wasn't only a symptom of cowardice and a sign that someone had something to hide. It could also be a way of showing consideration and compassion for others. She often forgot this now that he had passed, or she remembered it after it was too late. Hilda gave Walter care and affection with Mario and Gloria's help, but her skill was lacking when it came to gently educating Walter. She didn't have the patience to deal with him as a child.

When Walter turned eight, he began asking a lot of questions about the world. He started with race-based questions because he noticed his Great Auntie Gloria and his mother looked very different despite being related.

"Ma, why is Great Auntie Gloria's skin so much darker than yours?"

"Well, there are basically two kinds of Mexicans. There's the Spanishy-white looking kind and the Indian brownish kind." Even with her young son, Hilda didn't want to bother with political correctness.

"Why?"

"Because that's basically what Mexicans are, Indians that got colonized and raped by Spaniards."

"Oh, I think I get it a little." Walter didn't know what "rape" was but decided to save that question for later. "Am I white?" continued Walter.

"Sort of. Let's see. I'm half white and half Mexican and your father was half white and half Asian…so you're half white, a quarter Mexican and a quarter Asian."

Walter looked a little confused, mostly because it was a lot of information for a child to process.

"You're like a piece of Wonder Bread with some soy sauce and salsa on it," continued Hilda, making a failed attempt at explaining it better.

"That sounds really gross. I wouldn't eat that," said Walter, his face twisting up as he imagined the taste.

"You should probably say you're white," said Hilda.

"Why?"

"Because life can be easier when people think you're white or when you are white."

"Why?"

"Damnit Walter! You ask too many questions. It gets annoying. Go learn it yourself."

"I'm sorry, Ma," whimpered Walter.

Hilda felt guilty for losing her patience. She decided to cheer him up the way she always did.

"It's OK. You're my little Curious George and I love you."

She kissed him on the forehead and then tickled him until his smile returned. Hilda finished their little talk with something more rousing and positive. It was a version of a speech Eugene gave her when she expressed her concerns about her aunt judging her decision to marry a non-Latino man.

"Listen, Walt. In a few centuries, people are going to be so mixed up to the point where they won't bother with the basic colors anymore. There won't be white, brown, black and yellow. They'll be purple and orange and all shades of the rainbow. Maybe people will forget about colors because they'll be too many of them to bother with. It'll be too hard to hate people based on that anymore."

"That sounds good. I wanna be purple!"

Hilda smiled and patted his head.

As Walter grew older, he understood what it meant to be multiracial and began contemplating the choices that came with it. He learned people could identify only with one side or equally with both. Walter chose to identify with the different slices of his ethnic pie depending on the situation. When he was at the airport or pulled over by a cop, he was white. When his high school guidance counselor gave him college forms to fill out, he was Hispanic, "Two or more races," or "Other." When he wrote his college essay, he described all the different parts of his identity because he knew universities loved diversity. Nonetheless, Walter also loved the choice of being nothing as far as race was concerned. It was often relieving. In those cases, he was only Walter, a human being.

Walter also crafted his religious identity as he grew up or rather his lack of religious identity. It began, strangely enough, in first grade when he released a loud and smelly fart in class while the teacher was away for a minute. Most of the children laughed. The boy next to him was upset, not only because of his proximity to the putrescence, but also because his preacher father had scolded him earlier about flatulence.

"You shouldn't do that, Walter," said the boy.

"Why not?" replied Walter. "It's just a fart. They thought it was funny."

"Cuz God will get mad."

"Who's God?" Walter had not heard the term before. It was something Hilda had completely forgotten about because she worked on Sunday and let Walter sleep in. Walter looked around, thinking Mr. God might be one of the teachers or administrators and that he might be watching. There weren't any students in the class named "God." He began to fear this imaginary person was a big, bear-like man.

"You don't know what God is?" continued the boy, shocked at the discovery of a godless boy.

"It's a 'what?' It's not a person?"

"It's kind of a person," replied the boy. "He's this guy who lives up in the sky and watches everything and made everything. He judges and...and he doesn't like it when you fart," finished the boy, remembering where the conversation had begun.

"That sounds really dumb," said Walter, laughing at the concept and the images his mind had conjured, not aware of how sacred the idea of God could be. He couldn't help himself, though. He imagined a man sitting in a cloud and waving his hand in front of his nose rapidly as a putrid fart ascended past his domain and up into space. "Hot air rises" was one of his favorite little bits of trivia learned in school thus far.

The boy began to cry and tattled on Walter, resulting in a trip to the principal's office and a call to Hilda. She wasn't sure what to say to her son when he came home later that day. She believed in God, but only because Mario and Gloria had taught her to. She was ambivalent about religion because the memory of her parents attending church and pretending to be good, moral people still made organized religion unsavory. It hadn't occurred to her to take Walter to church.

She scolded him for being rude to the other child, explaining how belief in God was nothing to make fun of. Still, she told him he could decide his beliefs. He didn't need to believe in God or go to church.

———————

Hilda drifted from job to job as she raised Walter. Employers usually fired her for talking back, saying something inappropriate to the customers or losing her patience with male co-workers who flirted with her. She persevered through most of it, only occasionally displaying her frustration.

Walter caught her crying one time. She tried to stifle her sobs, but Walter was a light sleeper.

"What's wrong, Ma?" said Walter as he rubbed his eyes and walked from the bedroom they shared and into the living room of their tiny apartment. He put his hand on her shoulder while she tried to stop her tears. After a minute, she realized it wasn't so awful for her son to see her be vulnerable. He was getting into his teen years and was old enough to understand what she was going through.

"You know I always try my best, right Walt?"

"I know," replied Walter as he slid his hand gently up and down her back.

"There're just some things I can't help. I can't help who I am."

"I like who you are."

"Oh, honey." Hilda wiped her eyes with a tissue and then drew Walter in for a hug. They embraced warmly.

"Thank you. You're so sweet. I like me too. It's that 'me' gets in the way sometimes. I want us to have more money. I want you to be able to go to a nice school and have your own room."

"I don't mind sharing a room with you. I really don't."

"I'm so lucky to have a sweet, kind boy like you. You're like your Daddy."

She patted Walter on the back a few times as a signal it was time to let go. Walter had been conditioned to understand the action, so he promptly released her. Hilda blew her nose and finished drying her tears.

"Go to bed now, Walter," she said gently and lovingly, almost as a whisper.

Once she heard the bedroom door close, Hilda made an oath to herself and her son. She had been thinking about the decisions she'd make, the capabilities she had and how she might be able to make a better future for Walter. Although she had no regrets about marrying Eugene at a young age, she admitted it would've been ideal for both of them to go to college before conceiving a child. Since Eugene died she had only earned enough for them to survive and for Walter to eat somewhat healthily. She took advantage of the measly benefits the VA offered her as a military widow, but it wasn't nearly enough to save for a decent college education.

She had the option of leaving Walter in Gloria and Mario's care. They didn't have much more money than her, though. Hilda also didn't like the idea of relying on them again, not after all they had done for her.

Hilda knew how unlikely it was she would find a high paying job at the rate her career was going. She couldn't afford to take time off work and go to school either. At that moment Hilda resolved to save money for her son by whatever means necessary. She decided his future was worth more than her dignity and pride.

Walter made his own vow as he returned to their bedroom and nodded off to sleep. He would protect his mother and provide for her. He would save money for both of them and work hard. He would make sure she never had to cry again.

Three

Hilda was bartending for her latest job. Because bartenders could get away with being a bit abrasive, she expected to keep it longer than usual. Sometimes people condoned her behavior or believed it was necessary because customers constantly hit on her. Her rejections were a bit harsh, but the manager didn't mind. The customers came back. They were a thick-skinned bunch.

Walter was in high school now. He borrowed lots of books from the public library to satisfy his curiosity. He started with The Bible so he could attempt to understand more of what was going on in churches and what he might have been missing out on. The stories were fascinating and they had much more violence and sex than he expected. Reading something like The Bible felt oddly naughty to him, almost forbidden. By the time he finished it, he had more questions than answers. He wondered how much Christians actually followed it on average and pondered the circumstances under which it might have been written.

The accumulated knowledge and study habits helped him do well in school. Additionally, he used books to learn how to cook basic meals for himself and occasionally for his mother. This was part of Walter's plan because he wanted to avoid being a burden to his mother as much as possible. He figured if he did well in school and knew how to take care of himself, she would not have to work as much. It delighted Hilda. She was oblivious, however, to how much her continued wellbeing and stress reduction motivated Walter's efforts. She assumed Walter was performing well in school and learning life skills only for himself.

Hilda found what she believed to be Walter's ticket to a better future in the form of Michael Wallace, a wealthy man who was a regular at her bar. He was the chief engineer at a local military contracting company. He had worked vigorously and obtained the position at a young age. Michael had everything he wanted in life except for an attractive mate. Due to his success, he believed he was entitled to such a woman but had trouble dating due to his appearance. Bluntly put, he was ugly. He had a sort of upside down trapezoid for a head. His jaw was thin and almost feminine while the top of his head expanded like a mushroom. He had greasy hair and scars from acne during his teenage years.

He believed a woman could be obtained like other goals in life, as if it were not different than going after a job he wanted. Input would guarantee an output. His approach with women was direct and often aggressive. This method had allowed him to obtain everything else he had desired. All obstacles in his career had crumbled after he pushed hard enough. He rarely minced his words, believing that using euphemisms and fluffy words were a waste of time and a form of cowardice. Merciless honesty was sacred to him.

Naturally, women rejected him all the time. This caused him to accrue a lot of bitterness, almost to the point of hating the opposite sex. It became a vicious cycle because this bitterness led to even more rejection, frustration and anger.

Hilda's stomach turned at the clichéd idea of suckling money from a wealthy man. Nonetheless, she recognized it would be an easy and convenient way of providing for Walter. She approached Michael after her shift ended. He was heading for his Mercedes.

"Hey Mike. I have a proposition for you if you'll give me a moment."

"What it is?" asked Mike. He began fiddling with his keys while he waited for her to finish.

"I want you to give me some money to take care of my son and get him a good education. In return I'd go out on some dates with you, may be even a little more than that if you play your cards right."

Michael had become familiar with Hilda since he became a regular at the bar but was still surprised by how direct she could be.

"Ummm…let me think about it," replied Michael as he got in his car and started the engine.

Hilda smiled, confident he would accept. She had seen many women rebuke him and knew how desperate he was to have someone.

Michael was at the bar the next day. He knocked on the wooden counter to summon Hilda over. Like Hilda, Michael spoke openly and directly.

"How old is your son?" he began.

"Sixteen."

"Wow. You must've had him young. Either that or you're much older than you look."

"You're lucky I'm the kind of woman who appreciates honesty like that. I'm surprised you don't have a permanently red cheek from getting slapped all the time."

Michael laughed. The way she received his comments was refreshing.

"So are you trying to give me a 'Yes' to what I proposed to you the other day?" continued Hilda.

"You're very gorgeous and I like your attitude too. I'd definitely like to have you on my arm. The problem is it would be fake. I want to have a woman who isn't using me for my money. I want a woman who likes me for something other than that."

Hilda was tempted to say, "What else is there?" but decided to restrain herself for once. Walter's education was at stake.

"I'm sure you'll get that eventually. Then you can quit pretending with me and go for the new women who likes you for you. Why not pretend for now? It'll make you feel better and I need the money. It's mutually beneficial."

'That's a good point." Michael looked down at the Whiskey Ginger Hilda had mixed for him. He gyrated his hand a little and watched the liquid rotate in the glass. Then he looked back up at Hilda.

"Let's give it a try."

Four

Walter was happy to finally have his own room. He wondered where the money was coming from, though. As far as he could tell, his mother was still working her bartending job and nothing else. She had also been out more and was vague when Walter asked about it. Her usual responses were, "I'm going to dinner with a lady friend" or "Aren't I allowed to have some fun?" Walter didn't think too much about it for a while or rather was too busy for lengthy ponderings. He studied hard in school and spent his spare time reading and playing piano at weddings and other events with his school jazz combo. He also picked up a shift working the snack stands at the San Diego Zoo on Saturdays. His goal was still to make his mother proud and save enough money so she wouldn't have to burden herself with his education.

Walter also began to wonder what he might do with his life when he was older. He wasn't especially passionate about any one activity or career prospect. He was decent at piano playing, but only because he had practice and because the piano was the only instrument available to him without purchase or rental charges. The school pianos were open to everyone. Walter knew he had plenty of time to answer the "What are you going to do?" question adults were asking him. Still, he worried about it because he hadn't yet felt passion for an activity.

Hilda hated lying to her son but was initially satisfied with her and Michael's arrangement. He usually slipped her checks by putting them next to his credit card while he paid for drinks. The classic black envelope hid the checks and bundled them together. He then told her where he wanted to meet, what restaurant he wanted to take her to or what event for which he required her company. Hilda didn't think she was developing any feelings for him, but she did feel comfortable around him and thought she might consider him a friend someday. They had enough in common for their conversations to run smoothly.

Unbeknownst to Hilda, Michael was beginning to fall for her. He knew she was a widow and mistakenly believed she could let go of her attachment to a man who was nothing more than a memory.

After a few weeks of "dating," Michael decided to surprise Hilda by showing up at her apartment, the one he had helped her pay for. He knew where it was because he had dropped her off before. He rang the bell and fingered the necklace he had brought for her to ensure it was ready to be presented.

"Hi Hil…"

"What are you doing here?" interrupted Hilda. "I told you not to come here unless you're picking me up or dropping me off at certain times. You're lucky my son isn't home."

"I know you did and I'm sorry for going against that. I only wanted to surprise you with something."

"I'm not interested unless it's another check."

"Can you give me a few minutes Hilda? It's important." Hilda looked around and then checked the clock. She allowed him to speak his mind because Walter wouldn't be home for at least another hour.

"Go ahead," she said.

"All right then. I know this started as a way for you to get money and for me to build confidence and stroke my ego, maybe have someone on my arm to get attention and jealousy at events. I'm here to say I want it to be more than that. I don't want it to be fake anymore."

"So you want to date me without giving me money?" replied Hilda, already becoming impatient."

"I didn't mean that necessarily. I don't mind supporting you. It's easy for me. I only want this to be a real relationship as well." Hilda began to understand what he was saying.

"Look, Mike. I don't think you're a bad guy or anything, but I definitely don't like you as a boyfriend. If I decide to date someone again or get married,

I doubt it would be you. I'm not gonna give you any of that 'We can just be friends' BS or anything either. I like what we have going. Let's keep it that way."

"I thought we had good conversation. I thought we had things in common."

"Is that supposed to be special? Spending time with you isn't the worst thing in the world, but I think you're reading into it too much."

"So I'm just a checkbook to you. That's what I'm always going to be."

"I thought that's what our arrangement was. Now get lost before my son comes home. I'll see you later."

Michael's rage and bitterness made him shake. He stared into Hilda's cold expression. It only made him angrier. He tightened his fingers and slapped Hilda across the face with his right hand. She stumbled and nearly fell.

For an instant Michael was appalled and deeply ashamed of himself. He had not hit a woman before. Then he saw her face. It was red. She was shaking. This seemingly indestructible and iron-blooded woman was shaking. It was exhilarating for him. He felt empowered knowing he could inflict pain upon people who upset him.

Hilda feigned defeat and submission for a few seconds. Michael fell for the ruse and dropped his guard. He stopped shaking and exhaled slowly. As his gut relaxed and expanded, Hilda drove her fist into it as hard as she could. Michael fell to his knees and gasped for breath.

"If you want to hit me, then go ahead and hit me, you son of a bitch. Don't be surprised when I hit back."

Five

Walter and Hilda continued to drift further apart. They rarely had meals together because their schedules were different, and Walter could now take care of himself. Walter's worries about his mother didn't increase until he noticed a small bruise below her eye.

"How'd you get that?" he asked.

"Hit my head on the counter at work while I was reaching for some glasses."

Even the trusting and gullible Walter knew how terrible of a liar his mother was. Her lies were in sharp contrasts to her normal honesty. He wasn't sure if he should accuse her of lying or take action until he realized where the bruises were coming from.

"Hey, Mom."

"What's up, honey?"

"You can tell me what's really going on if you want. I won't be mad. I'm old enough to understand."

Hilda set down the laundry she was organizing. She stared at the floor and formulated a response.

"I'm a grown woman, Walter. I know what I'm doing. You're my son. It's not your job to worry about me."

"I just don't want you to get hurt, Mom. I know I can't tell you what to do. I don't want you to get hurt anymore. That's all."

"I'm fine. If I really start getting hurt, I can stop what I'm doing anytime I want."

"What are you doing?"

"I told you it's none of your business." Hilda slammed the door to her bedroom, which was now completely hers. Walter knew she was being abused but didn't know any of the specific details. It also puzzled him. He couldn't imagine his mother allowing anyone to hit her more than once. Still, he assumed it was a man she was dating. Even the imaginative Walter could not formulate any other scenario that made sense.

The biggest clue came when Walter noticed her leave the house late at night. She exited swiftly but still gave Walter a second-long window to watch her. He snuck around the corner without a sound so he could catch a glimpse before she opened the door and walked out. She had an expensive-looking dress on and high heels, items of clothing he had not seen her wear before. Hilda didn't care for aesthetics. Clothing was no exception.

"Don't waste your energy on girls who are only good at looking pretty. They won't have much else to offer."

"I don't get why women wear high-heels. They're painful as hell. Only stupid, shallow guys are gonna value something like that."

His mother's wisdom rung in his ears as he processed the conflicting information. Walter had only seen her in cheap jeans and t-shirts until that night.

She returned from the party with a fresh bruise on her cheek, courtesy of her latest altercation with Michael. As she ran her hand along it, her body tingled as the memory of the fight ran through her mind. Her heart beat accelerated and her swollen cheeks flushed. The adrenaline was thrilling, vaguely pleasurable. She began to weep quietly, disgusted and horrified by how her time with Michael was threatening to completely mutate her values and personality.

After drying her tears, she restored her resolve as she always did. It was a three-step routine that had not failed. First, she looked at a picture of Walter and herself that Gloria had taken recently. Then she thought about how her aunt had been right to push for a college education and how she didn't want Walter to make the same mistakes she did. Lastly, she tallied up the money from her checks and compared it to the minimum amount needed for four years at a University of California college.

Despite her attempts to hide it, her son noticed the new bruise. The heavy use of makeup was another oddity for Hilda. It drew attention despite the cover it provided. For Walter this was the last piece of evidence he needed to deduce that his mother was in some sort of abusive relationship. He ruminated upon what he could do to protect her. After some deliberation, he decided he would have to confront the man himself if she wouldn't leave him. Walter wasn't confident he could do it, though. He wasn't particularly strong and had not been in a fight before.

The answer came when he remembered how he had accomplished most of his other goals. It was all about indulging his curiosity and then using the knowledge to gain power. It helped him cook, it helped him do well in school and now it would help him learn to fight. It would, of course, be a last resort.

Walter began training but still periodically urged his mother to change her lifestyle. He even became more direct and made statements such as "You can leave him anytime you want." Hilda simply pushed on and ignored Walter. Nonetheless, she did begin keeping track of how much money she saved, referencing it with estimates of four years of tuition for decent colleges. Once she became closer to her estimate, she would cease her arrangement with Michael. The problem was that it would be at least a year more. She wasn't sure how much longer she could handle it with without sustaining permanent damage.

Hilda considered terminating her agreement with Michael before she saved enough money. She worried if she quit, however, she might not be able to find another way of earning extra money for Walter. It would also be difficult because Michael was a regular at the bar where she worked and she couldn't afford to quit her job.

Walter began his training by lifting weights every day at the school gym. He also joined the afterschool martial arts club. Learning self-defense for the purpose of intimidating someone was wrong and Walter knew this. Nonetheless, he maintained that rescuing his mother was far more important. Walter also began heading home at different times without telling Hilda so he could learn when the mystery abuser dropped her off. He stayed out of sight so his mother wouldn't notice and then hung out at a local diner until it became time for his expected arrival at home.

Although he was confident his physical training would pay off, Walter still worried about how he would fare. He initially hesitated due to his moral reservations about fighting. The kind boy had not been in a fight before. The thought of hurting someone, even in defense of his mother, made him uncomfortable at first.

The mere concept of a fight disturbed him as well. Any sort of conflict usually resulted in winners and losers, whether it was a war between nations or a brawl between thugs. A considerate person would avoid conflict unless absolutely necessary. But what circumstances made conflict necessary? Walter reaffirmed his decision after realizing that inaction carried the risk of his mother's death and that any such risk, no matter how small, prompted action. The fact that this man was remotely likely to kill his mother made the conflict necessary.

The other element of his training was mental rehearsal. He imagined all the different ways the confrontation might go, the sound of his fist breaking a nose, the rush of adrenaline, the blood loss. The visualizations became addicting. They excited him and pleasured him at times. He began to experience rewards from these fantasies as if they were actually happening. The reservations and apprehension about harming his opponent began to subside. He severely underestimated how powerful his mind was. He started having nightmares about the fight where he murdered the man in question. This horrified Walter. He wondered if the research and mental simulations were poisoning him with bloodlust and morbid curiosity, adding a rapidly growing element that wasn't there before and wasn't meant to be there, much like an invasive species. Or maybe it was there from the beginning and the mental rehearsal for the fight was merely unearthing such violent desires.

The situation reminded Walter of a story he had read after picking up a collection from the local library. It was about a man who, after seeing his stove malfunction, developed anxieties about his house catching on fire and burning to a pile of charred wood and ashes. Even after having the stove thoroughly repaired and doubly inspected, the thought still consumed him. It infected his dreams and tortured him at work, forcing him to run home and check the stove. He began obsessing over it, repeatedly visualizing all the different ways the house might burn down, playing every image and detail on a loop in his mind: how the fire would cause all his files to curl up in fetal positions as they burned, the glory of the explosion once the gas pipe reacted with the flames, the orange glow against the night sky. Eventually, this drove him insane. He believed the only way to rid himself of the nightmares was to burn his house down so his curiosity would be satisfied. The crazed man started the fire in the kitchen by tampering with his stove. He retreated from it, soon exiting his house so he wouldn't be harmed. As he watched unimpressive smoke silently escape from the windows, unable to see anything more, he realized his mistake: reality rarely had the ability to surpass or even rival imagination. Firemen came and squelched the flames before the gas explosion could occur. The man finally ceased his fantasies, vowing to never again indulge his mind past the point of reason.

Even this final sign of caution was not enough to deter Walter. Like his mother, he resolved to move forward with his plan and ignore the trepidations.

The confrontation came when Walter decided to arrive home early so he could ambush the mysterious lover as he dropped off Hilda. Walter waited next to the living room window so he could see them coming. Instead of dropping her off as he normally did, Michael parked the car and followed Hilda into the apartment. Walter scrambled into his bedroom, fearing he might have to hide for now and try another day. He hadn't anticipated the man coming into the apartment. It wasn't part of the plan.

Hilda and Michael's altercation grew louder as they approached the door. Walter could hear it clearly once they entered.

"My son is going to be home soon. Don't do this, Mike. I'm warning you."

Michael shoved his way into the apartment. Walter peered around the corner and saw the man clearly for the first time. He noticed bruises on his mother's alleged lover as well. This was confusing, but it also made Walter feel a little better to know his mother was at least fighting back.

"I pay for most of this shit," replied Michael. "I should be able to come in here. In a way, I own you too." Michael tried to put his arms around Hilda restrain her. He groped her breasts for a moment as she pushed him away. The idea of being owned struck a chord with Hilda.

"You think you're special? You think there aren't a million other ugly, rich motherfuckers out there?"

"Why haven't you left then? You must like something about it, you sick bitch."

"That's it. We're done. Don't come any closer, Mike."

"Leave then. I paid for this place. If we're done, then you're leaving with me. Or you can leave and I can stay." He advanced again, trying to grope her.

"Don't come any closer, Mike. We're done. I don't need your money anymore if it's gonna be like this."

"I'm not leaving before I wreck you, you miserable cunt!"

"Enough!" screamed Walter as he leapt from around the corner.

Both Michael and Hilda were shocked. Michael had never seen Walter before and Hilda was petrified by the humiliation of Walter seeing her in such a predicament.

"You need to leave now," continued Walter. "No one talks to my Mom that way. I don't want to see your face again. You're never gonna see my Mom again either."

Michael broke free from his shock, but Hilda was still frozen.

"He doesn't know about any of it, does he?" said Michael, laughing. "I'll give you the short version. Your mother's a whore. I paid for this place and that room you get all to yourself. All of this is mine, so I'm not leaving until I feel like it."

Walter was terribly confused. He still hadn't completely figured out the arrangement his mother had with Michael. Even Michael didn't know that the vast majority of his money was for Walter's education. He assumed Hilda was hording it for herself. This fueled his already burgeoning anger. He'd become a beast now, consumed by bitterness and frustration.

"My mom and I can sort out the details later," said Walter. "You need to leave right now. I'll make you if you don't." Michael folded his arms and stared at Walter. Walter understood this signal and bore down on him, ready to begin the fight.

Walter started with a jab to the nose. Michael pushed Walter's fist aside so its course diverted. He hadn't trained the way Walter had but did have a bit of experience from fighting with Hilda. The blow swiped his cheekbone rather than striking his nose. Walter's fingers ached a bit from the bones colliding, but not nearly enough to make him hesitate. It was easy to ignore the pain. Adrenaline was surging through his body, working in conjunction with his desire to continue the fight, to win, to protect his mother. Sweat burst out of him as if it had broken through a dam. Subconscious fear was pushing it out. He realized that all his mental preparation could not match the actual event. His mind was not powerful enough to simulate the intense emotions that arose during a fight.

Michael countered with a hook. Walter dodged it for the most part but it still smacked the tip of his lip, causing it to bleed. Walter did not see the blood, though, or realize had lost it. He charged at Michael and tackled him to the floor. He ignored the blows Michael tried to rain down on his back and quickly went for the face while it was unguarded.

Walter wrapped his legs around Michael's torso as tightly as he could so his opponent couldn't wriggle away. He struck him in the face several more times until Michael's arms slowed down. Walter ceased his assault for a second as he noticed tears welling up in the man's eyes. The liquid evoked sympathy, even in the middle of the brawl. Walter wondered what had happened to him, what had caused him to be abusive. His opponent suddenly appeared so pitiful.

Walter almost stopped the attack until he remembered why he had begun. This man had harmed his mother. He would continue to do so unless he was taken down, humiliated in such a way that he would be too afraid to try again. More selfishly, his subconscious spurred him on, realizing this might be the only chance to sublimate his violent urges. Walter struck him again and again until he had forgotten about his sympathy, until he had bludgeoned away all of his foe's consciousness. He became enamored with the moment, indulging in too much ecstasy for the thought of murder to register. The pleasure of dominance squelched any rationality.

Hilda finally took action and laid her hands on Walter's shoulders, hoping to pry him off. Walter cast her off reflexively and with considerable force, causing her to stumble backwards a few paces and land on the coffee table. Her back broke the table and the pieces of wood cut her arms and back. The cuts were shallow, hardly worth a hospital visit but still painful. The sound of the wood breaking woke Walter from his trance. He ceased his barrage and rushed over to his mother.

"Don't," screamed Hilda as he approached. She was crying again. It was like the last time Walter saw her cry. He tried taking another step until she screamed again.

"Don't come near me! I mean it!" She threw the nearby lamp at Walter.

"Mom, please. You're bleeding. Let me help you. It's my fault. I didn't mean to hurt you."

"It was all for you! All of this shit!" continued Hilda as she raised herself up from the wreckage of the table. "You think I'm that weak? You think I can't take a few hits? Why? Why did you have to do this? Damn it! Damn it! Fuck!!" She wept harder. Walter still didn't fully understand what she meant.

"We don't need more money, Mom. I'm working hard. I'll take care of us and pick up the slack." Hilda shook her head in response.

"I fucked up," she said to herself. "I'm so stupid."

Walter tried one last time to comfort her. She pushed him away this time instead of shouting. She was equally upset with herself. Hilda wanted to crawl away in a hole so she never had to face her son. She believed she had failed as a mother. The humiliation and shame was unbearable. Furthermore, Walter had frightened her. He had instilled fear she hadn't felt since those tall men in suits arrived to take her parents away.

"Go to Gloria's house," said Hilda.

"But Ma…"

"I'm not going to say it again. Go! I started this. I'll clean it up. Do what I say, Walter."

Walter began crying as well. He walked slowly towards the door and looked back toward his mother before he left.

"I love you, Mom, and I'm sorry."

She didn't respond. She wanted to be left alone.

———

In Hilda's mind, she was no longer worthy to be Walter's mother. She sent him to live with Gloria and Mario for the remainder of his senior year of high school. She supported him financially but almost completely repudiated him in every other element of their relationship. Walter received checks in the mail with letters explaining how he was supposed to use the money and how Hilda still loved him despite their distance.

It broke Walter's heart. He never completely forgave himself for handling the situation the way he did. He only saw his mother two more times in his life: once at his college graduation and once at his wedding.

Hilda's life actually improved after her falling out with Michael. She handled the aftermath quickly by returning a portion of his money and urging him not to press charges against her son. Right before she quit her job at the bar, another regular customer approached her and offered her a job as radio talk show co-host. He loved the way she spoke so honestly and bluntly about popular topics. He said she would be hilarious on the radio and there was a perfect spot for her. Shortly afterward, she was "Hot-Ice Hilda" at 98.1 FM.

Walter continued to drift through life without a focus. He loved learning but could not manage to find a single subject, activity or career he wanted to dedicate himself to. He fell into a deep depression after his mother left and only managed to heal once he found Susan.

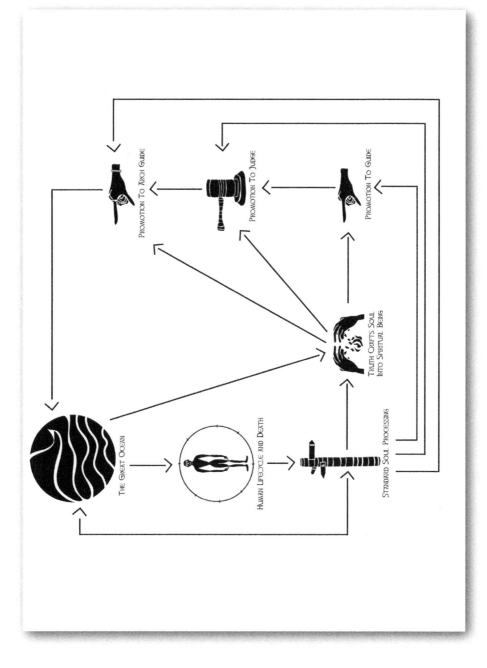

Part V

One

For centuries, The Truth was nameless or rather there wasn't any sort of consistent name. The Truth did not find it important to insist upon one. This changed when man invented the singular and all-powerful God.

Souls who believed in this idea of God, especially the ones who created and popularized this idea, conflated The Truth with God during their time in the afterlife. They would cry out to it, pray to it, weep in front of it and rejoice that their faith was now justified. They didn't understand that The Truth had not created the universe, nor the Earth, nor man. It had no power over anything physical, only souls. It was merely an observer of the physical world. The Truth had to repeatedly explain to these souls that it wasn't God. Eventually, The Truth required guides to educate each soul about its nature and how it was different from God, instructing them to instill a cautious optimism in their souls regarding the existence of a true God. The Truth wanted those with faith to keep it, but also for them to understand the situation outside the context of their beliefs.

The Truth struggled with the idea of a being with the ability to create matter. After all, it had not consciously created spiritual matter nor had it crafted the first unique human soul. It was a manager and crafter of spiritual matter that had mimicked natural occurrences rather than creating them. It was like an artist painting a replication of an original work. It had no memory of willing any souls into existence. Rather, the souls were simply there, ready for The Truth to manage them. It had no idea where they came from.

Although The Truth sometimes wanted to validate human beliefs, it could not provide faithful souls with any evidence of God. Furthermore, it had witnessed the creation of man and knew that a being had not placed humans upon the earth. Souls who believed God had crafted man with his hands were simply wrong. The Truth decided to allow people to hold these beliefs through the afterlife. It seemed unnecessary and cruel to prove them wrong and rob them of the happiness these beliefs provided. Thus, The Truth made a rule that people could profess their beliefs, religious or not, in the afterlife so long as they did not use them to discriminate and insult others. Souls that attempted to harass others because of differences in ideology, gender, religion, sexual orientation and race were temporarily removed from processing and sometimes given extra punishments. The guides educated these bigoted souls until they either reformed their beliefs, agreed they would not misbehave or until they made it clear that they would not cease. If the latter occurred, the guide sent the soul immediately to nothingness without a trial. This rule designed to promote tolerance was one of the oldest in the spiritual processing system and managed to endure despite many sweeping changes through the centuries.

The difficulty was reconciling modern standards of human morality with the more highly evolved conclusions The Truth had come to using its superior intellect. The Truth did not always blame humans for being homophobic or anti-Semitic. Larger times and culture dictated beliefs, swallowing up the individual and robbing it of its chance to come to a fair and unbiased conclusion. "Humans should judge humans" could be a dangerous notion because it meant dooming innocent people based on predispositions. As a way to compensate for this, The Truth created multiple systems where people within communities could judge one another. This delayed the issue of discrimination considerably and became standard practice until man's moral reasoning evolved sufficiently.

As these afterlife communities grew along with the earth's population, an increasing number of guides demanded a standard name so they could unanimously reference the ruler of the spiritual realm without confusion. The first group of guides The Truth molded, the ones from deceased souls or pure souls who had never touched the physical realm, saw their crafter as a great arbiter, an absolute source of information.

The Truth struggled with a name at first. It wanted something that felt powerful and carried authority without sounding like God. It wanted something versatile. Truth meant despair. Truth meant beauty. Truth meant brutality. Truth meant no mercy. Truth meant respecting someone enough to privilege him or her with fact. Truth meant the complete truth. Complete truth meant complete observation.

Humans could not obtain complete truth. Even if they could, it would be beyond their comprehension. Even if a man could understand and absorb the complete truth for a moment, it would destroy him. Thus, the nameless being took on its new mantle and became "The Truth."

Two

As for how it began, The Truth came into existence as a set of beings acting as arbiters of souls for all living creatures. Unlike many of its siblings, it was not tasked with processing souls for a certain species immediately after its birth. It was doomed to drift for centuries as nothing but a ghostly omnipresence, devoid of purpose. It begged its siblings to allow it to help in processing souls, but they refused, claiming it would be a violation of their duty.

It passed the time by wandering and observing the Earth with its myriad eyes until it had seen every inch of the planet a thousand times and grown tired of watching other species evolve and repeat the same basic behaviors of replicating, fighting, eating and sleeping. Only time had the power to rob the Earth of its wonder.

The Truth wanted a species capable of intellect, a species that could observe, evolve and ask the same questions it was asking: What more is there to this planet? What can be accomplished beyond mere survival?

Answers to these questions did not arrive for millions of years. The boredom and emptiness became excruciating. It wished it could become nothing. It wished it could disappear or die or fall into a deep sleep and be woken once it had a purpose.

Just when it began seeking a way to end its existence, it felt a piece of energy flowing into its core. Then it felt another piece being removed. Its brethren had described the sensation, but The Truth had not felt it before. They described themselves as metaphysical containers of water. Rain dripped out of them, producing a tingle. Eventually, this same liquid would return in a different form and then revert to its original state as it entered the body of water. The Truth slowly discovered this was the process of souls migrating to their bodies and then back to The Truth once the body had died. For The Truth, the body of pure souls appeared as a blue ocean suspended in a white sky. It was a spherical ocean with clearly defined boundaries. It expanded and contracted as humans perished and thrived. The total volume did not change, though. The Truth could see it beating inside itself like a heart while still being able to view it and control it.

When souls exited the great ocean inside The Truth, the outside environment corrupted their pure nature, causing them to mutate in an infinite number of different ways and develop idiosyncrasies as they rushed to inhabit a body in the physical realm. These mutations intensified as the soul neared the body. A rainbow of wavelengths beyond human perception consumed the pure blue until it bore no resemblance to its original form. The Truth eventually learned to see these seemingly disgusting mutations as the cherished process of making each soul distinct. No two souls were exactly the same after they finished mutating, even if they appeared incredibly similar. They were like drops of water or falling snow. Souls continued to change as they inhabited bodies of flesh because each new experience and emotion furthered the beautiful mutations.

When souls left their dead bodies and returned to the great ocean, they purified. They blended in with the rest of the pure blue and became blank once again, unfeeling and inexperienced. The barrier cast off the mutations that had formed around the pure blue and disintegrated them. The process of recycling finished and the souls were ready to be sent to the physical realm and mutated once more.

The Truth continued to observe man but was still unable to differentiate its behavior and purpose from other species. Man had evolved, but its behavior still only consisted of basic survival such as hunting and mating. The Truth grew impatient again until a monumental day when it watched an early human excitedly rubbing rocks together. The Truth could not understand what it was trying to accomplish until it saw sparks rain onto the ground. The embers smoldered on the ground and evolved until flames consumed the grass. The early human leapt in fear and admiration for the fire and shouted with pride from its accomplishment. This shouting alerted his tribe. They gathered around the flame, bringing their hands as close to it as they could without bathing them in the expanding inferno.

The Truth marveled after piecing together its recordings of life on Earth, realizing it had already witnessed the humble beginnings of man. It traced back the recordings as far as it was able to and watched a hapless fish crawl onto a beach, somehow managing to breathe.

Upon seeing the origins of man and the great intellectual potential the species had, The Truth began taking great pride in its duty, boasting to its brethren that it had been tasked with the greatest species. Although it could not see into the future, it had grand hopes for man. It watched the process of spiritual mutation and recycling unfold with newfound pleasure.

Three

The Truth was content to let this relatively simple process play out until it observed humans developing a sense of morality and complex emotions. The Truth first incubated the idea of rewarding and punishing souls after watching an early human charge into a peaceful tribe, bludgeon a man to death, and then run off with his mate. The kidnapped mate refused sex with him, so he bludgeoned her to death as well.

As The Truth's many eyes hovered over her body, it wished it had the power to physically intervene. Sight and sound were the only senses it could use to absorb the stimuli of the physical world. The Truth crafted an invisible and intangible form so it could sit beside her body as a ghostly vessel.

"If I could smell and feel like the humans do, I would be nauseous by now," it thought. "Flies are already gathering around her."

"If I could feel her skin with human hands, I would cringe as the layers of dirt blemished my fingers. Humans are disgusting and impure, both physically and spiritually. Yet, there is something amazing about them. They have the intellectual ability to achieve and suffer more than any other species. They are capable of unrivaled kindness and cruelty. Despite this, their physical existence is so frail, limited and unjust."

"This woman was innocent. She was a kind mother. I wish my touch could raise her up again so she could watch her children become men and women. This is why physical life is so cruel. Everything is determined by chance. The wicked have as much chance to prosper as the kind-hearted. People reward evil deeds and many humans are born without the ability to enjoy the world.

Some don't live long enough to know who they are or have a chance to be happy."

"They've started inventing these Gods and deities, telling others to believe in them. I'm not exactly sure why, but I have some theories. To accept the fact that there is no divine governance and justice in the world is unbearably depressing for some. Humans would rather believe there are sentient forces controlling the Earth, giving reasons to the harshest realities, accounting for what they have yet to understand. I know better than anyone that humans' existence on Earth has no guiding hand, that luck is the most powerful and unbiased force on the planet. Its nature is not to deliver justice."

"Perhaps I'm projecting my own frustration on humans. Why was I given these unlimited observational powers without the ability to intervene? Why must I only watch their spirits flow? I care about them. I'll admit that. Their emotions and desire for justice has infected me. This infection has remained no matter how much I've tried to dilute it. Then again, perhaps that is a negative way of perceiving my transformation. Maybe I am evolving along with them, extrapolating ideas from their actions and processing them at an exponentially faster rate than the humans themselves."

"I only want to help them. Watching the good ones die with so much left to do fills me with sadness. Seeing the wicked prosper and enter the great ocean without consequences for their actions makes me furious. I don't know how much longer I can stand by. Sometimes I think I would rather fade out of existence than remain powerless."

Meanwhile, The Truth's other eyes watched her soul approach the great ocean. This time, it halted before entering the sphere and casting off its mutations. Its comet-like form changed as its movement ceased. It transformed into a sort of orb. The Truth wondered if its desires had brought about this new development.

For the first time, it could touch a human, not physically but spiritually. As its fingers gently touched the surface of the orb, it entered the spiritual body like a bee perching upon a flower. It could feel her existence. Her pain and desires became tangible. The Truth began testing the limits of its power by seeing if its will could shape her soul. Instantly, the orb swelled with false memories of the life she had wanted: peace among tribes, nothing but days of play and rest with her children and mate, some hunting challenges but nothing where anyone died.

The Truth was elated with the realization that it had power over the spiritual domain. By flexing its abilities, it strived to evolve into a being that could balance the injustices of the physical world by giving the righteous what the material world had deprived them of and punishing the wicked so luck would only save them until death, not for eternity.

The man who took the innocent woman's life escaped. He lived a short and happy life without punishment, dying a peaceful death with no consequences from his actions.

As it had done before, its many eyes bore down on the soul as it neared the pure ocean. As The Truth focused its anger, the soul halted before it hit the cleansing barrier. Its gaseous form suspended. The Truth then discovered it could induce experiences such as torture. During the torture, The Truth learned it could modify souls. It could mold them like clay and dissect them like a surgeon, removing unwanted parts, learning that certain colors and textures corresponded to behaviors, beliefs and tendencies. The Truth continued to use souls who had sinned greatly in the physical realm as test subjects while bestowing pleasurable experiences upon good souls or at least allowing them to reach the ocean without incident. This became the foundation for the soul processing system The Truth would eventually develop. It felt pangs of guilt during the experiments but decided the sinners' suffering was a fitting price for acquiring knowledge.

The next step was configuring the structure and metaphysics of the spiritual realm. The Truth learned quickly that normal human souls had trouble abandoning the laws of the physical world. Using their spiritual bodies and directly interacting with the spiritual realm was incredibly difficult for most souls. The Truth solved this problem by giving each incoming soul the ability to perceive the spiritual world as they did the physical world. The spiritual world had a series of complex codes that only The Truth was able to decipher after centuries of trial and error. Each code corresponded to a different simulated experience or property.

It was similar to how simple front-end web development worked. When people use a website, they see the structure and aesthetics the codes have produced. They see something useable and familiar. If someone with absolutely no knowledge of web development were to take a look under the hood of a website, the languages and lines of code would appear as nothing more than random strings of letters and symbols, awkwardly formatted and littered about. Someone with programming experience, however, would read it as if it were a spoken language. This person would see the elegance and beauty of the seemingly drab lines of code. Unfortunately, the programming language of the spiritual realm was too complicated for most humans to tap into.

The Truth attempted to manage the system alone until it began suffering from the spiritual equivalent of stress headaches. It desperately searched for a way to relieve the pain without relinquishing its absolute control but could not do so. Its brethren offered to take some of the burden, but it repudiated them out of spite because they had not allowed it a purpose during its centuries of boredom.

To relieve stress, The Truth created a spiritual processing system where other beings would manage the incoming souls to an extent. It used its skill in molding souls to take pure forms from the great ocean of souls and mold them into spiritual beings with artificial memories, giving them duties as guides and judges. It also intercepted souls bound for recycling if it believed their earthly experience would make them suited for assistance in spiritual processing. Even if their origins differed, The Truth usually implanted some artificial memories into spiritual beings to serve various purposes. These newly created spiritual beings served The Truth indefinitely. The Truth replaced some upon request or following a poor performance review. Nonetheless, it would only grant requests if it was satisfied with their service. Each judge and guide received training so they could access the spiritual realm directly and understand the code that birthed the experiences normal human souls perceived. Spiritual beings could manipulate the code to an extent but had only a modicum of power over it compared to The Truth. This ability allowed them to guide human souls, keep them in line and observe them in the physical world.

The Truth and its spiritual beings then worked together to construct organized systems of courtrooms and waiting rooms. It was much like a team of developers building a complex website. Once it was finished, The Truth generally left the spiritual beings to manage and maintain it. It allowed the judges to propose punishments but kept the duty of administering rewards entirely to itself. It also distilled the amount of information judges could view to make proceedings more efficient. Guides had less authority than judges but could be promoted or given special rewards if they demonstrated outstanding insight.

The Truth often reflected fondly on some of the first cases where the court system functioned well. One of its favorites was that of a soul who had stolen a vial of medicine.

"I only did it to help my mother!" he pleaded.

"Yes, but you took the last vial that was in stock. Another sickly person died because of your theft, because there was no more medicine. I have the facts right here, straight from The Truth," retorted the judge.

"I realize that and I'm deeply sorry for it. I did not know it was the last vial. Had I known, I wouldn't have taken it."

"This is true, but a sin is a sin and theft is one I take seriously. You will receive a punishment, but it will not be so harsh. I was thinking of having you watch the fate of the patient who died without the available medicine, the grieving of his family and how they went on without him. I also want you to experience your own mother's death, which would've happened had you not stolen. Hopefully The Truth will approve both of these suggestions. That is all."

Before the soul could interject, his guide took him firmly be the shoulder and shook his head, instructing him not to argue unless he wanted a more severe punishment. The soul complied and walked silently toward post-judgment.

The Truth watched proudly like a parent standing by as its child took its first steps without hands inches away, waiting to cradle it after it fell.

The next step was deciding how to deal with souls after they had been judged. For centuries, The Truth stuck with its method of giving each individual a unique fantasy based on his or her sins, desires and memories. It was compelled, however, to begin experimenting with alternatives after humans created the idea of "heaven," a space where good souls lived together in peace and pleasure. Thus, The Truth created a utopian world with no disease, aging, hatred, poverty, or conflict, a place where only the kindest souls could enter. Resources were unlimited and pollution was non-existent. Each soul retained memories of life in the physical realm and had access to the same homes, resources, and activities. They could mingle as they pleased, relax, indulge in delicious but healthy food, and live their lives free of work and struggle. It was a sort of eternal vacation.

At first, souls expressed immense satisfaction. The Truth surveyed them regularly by either reaching out telepathically or taking a human form and wandering the heavenly space. It only took a year for complaints to become common. After a decade, nearly all of the original residents of the Truth's Eden had some sort of existential grievance.

"I'm horribly bored. It's wonderful here and I'm grateful, but it's so limiting. I've already run out of things to do. I've done the same activities thousands of times."

"I want to see my family and friends. Why did you leave me with memories of them even though I might have to wait decades to see any of them? I don't think I can be happy here without them."

"I want to be able to work. Work was what made me happy before. Now I can't do it. Please let me go back. Or maybe you could give me another experience where I can work?"

"There was so much I wanted to do before I died. Could you allow me to ex-perience those things? I can't find them here. It's not the same."

"It's been so long here or at least it feels that way. My daughter must've passed on by now. I never got to meet her, so I would love to see her if possible. Did she grow up to be a sinner? Is that why she isn't here?"

Due to the volume of complaints, spiritual beings started describing it as a glorified retirement home, a running joke that irritated The Truth. But with-out death and age, retirement lost its value. No retirement could be desirable if it was forced and permanent, if there was no flesh to age. The shared and eternal heaven model was also not sustainable. The Truth knew it would even-tually need to recycle these souls as Earth's population grew and increased the demand for new souls. It also realized the shortcomings of a world with only bliss and comfort. The idea of an Eden robbed "goodness" of its value because its creators did not realize that people appraise their situations based on relativity and opposites. Goodness became nothingness because evil did not exist. Without strife and struggle, many souls could not value their privileges. The concept of a personal or shared heaven void of sin was merely a sweet sound, a single note held forever rather than a melody. Like any tone, no matter how beautiful, listening to it for an extended period of time became a curse if the sound did not deviate from its origin.

To remedy these problems and prevent future complaints, The Truth returned to its use of individualized heaven experiences. The Truth deduced that, despite popular depictions of heaven found in religious texts and communities, most people did not want a second life that was mostly or entirely detached from their first. They actually wanted a modified version of their life on Earth, one where they could retain their memories to experience new events, meet different people, make different choices and appreciate what they could not before. Despite the evolution of human imagination and desire, in spite of all the grand visions of the afterlife, the spirit of that innocent early human woman lived on in every person. It was the simple desire for reparations, the longing to have the afterlife provide what the physical realm did not.

People who died young wanted to live longer. People who passed from sickness or lived with disabilities wanted to experience a life free of these limitations while keeping their memories of strife so every new moment in their fantasy became wonderful by comparison. Slaves wanted to travel through the same world as free men and women. Gay men and women wanted to live in a version of Earth where their lifestyle would not be condemned. A shared heaven could offer them these experiences, but they were only meaningful in the context of their former lives.

Following similar logic, The Truth began its reform of the shared hell it had created along with heaven. From its inception, the main criticism was that it was too harsh, even for the most heinous of sinners. For centuries, the punishments were derived from religious texts, mythology, lore and torture/execution methods from various cultures throughout time. Initially, The Truth designed hell to be eternal, a place where souls would continuously suffer their punishments, receiving few breaks.

This was short lived. The Truth pitied these souls and decided such methods were extreme. The next version of a shared hell was a nearly empty space that, to its inmates, appeared to continue for infinity. The Truth then populated it with resources and weapons so the souls of hell had something to fight over. This created an environment where simply existing was a form of punishment. Even this version, however, had the same issues of soul sustainability and became insufficient as humans evolved on Earth and developed a more complex sense of morality.

Once again, individualized experiences were more popular among most souls and spiritual beings. These punishments generally did not run the risk of being excessive and were not designed to be eternal, solving the issue of sustainability by allowing more souls to be recycled. After all, every soul in existence was destined to return to its original state no matter how much time it spent in heaven or hell. Every soul eventually shed its mutations gained from unique experiences and took its place in the pure ocean, ready to start the journey again once a different body called out to it.

Four

The system began without a Right of Choice. The Right of Choice did not come about until The Truth observed existential philosophy in the physical realm. Upon studying this philosophy and remembering its own desire for nothingness during its centuries of mind-numbing boredom when it lacked a purpose, The Truth began giving worthy souls the choice between nothingness and fantasy. The option was unpopular, but the rare souls who chose it kept it alive.

The nothingness souls chose wasn't true nothingness. Nothingness didn't exist. It was only an idea. Many humans assumed choosing nothingness meant their souls would be completely destroyed rather than being recycled. Nonetheless, it only felt that way because the dive into the great ocean provided a final cleansing process that stripped the mutated souls of their impurities. Like physical matter, spiritual matter could not be created or destroyed. It simply existed as far as The Truth knew. It could only be transformed and moved, not extinguished.

Souls who chose nothingness believed they were reaching an exclusive destination when, in fact, they were only taking a different route to the same great ocean traveled by all beings. The Truth had trouble deciding whether it should inform souls of this limitation in the system. It had tried in vain to create and destroy spiritual matter and had failed repeatedly to the point of giving up. The matter only broke into infinitesimal pieces that would eventually regroup or find their way back to the great ocean. Souls rarely asked about this in enough detail to realize the true nature of the choice. The Truth, however, had instructed guides and judges to lie about the nature of the choice so it would not become less appealing to those invested in it.

The Truth once wondered if this was necessary. It considered that maybe the mutations and idiosyncrasies formed around the soul were the only properties that defined it, that each pure soul from the great ocean did not have any unique innate qualities. Perhaps stripping the soul down to its purity was a form of nothingness.

The issue of the number of souls being finite also beguiled The Truth. It had counted during its centuries of boredom. There were exactly ten billion. This number did not change. The location of the souls and their forms only shifted. The Truth wondered what this meant for the fate of humanity. Would all children be stillborn and soulless if the Earth's population exceeded ten billion? Would these stillborn children be given souls every time another person died? Why was it ten billion? Was there a higher being that created the great ocean and decided on this number?

The Truth pursued the answers to these questions relentlessly. It wondered if it had a creator and if that creator had one as well. It wondered how far the chain of creation went or if there was one to begin with. After seeing how humans had evolved from almost nothing, The Truth followed the assumption that it had done the same in a past life. The Truth was happy that humans had introduced such ideas. Meanwhile it continued improving and expanding its spiritual processing system.

One of the newest additions to the system was rewarding spiritual beings for analyzing the rationale behind souls with a "Special Focus." Now it was focused on a man named Walter Klein for reasons most of the spiritual beings could not discern.

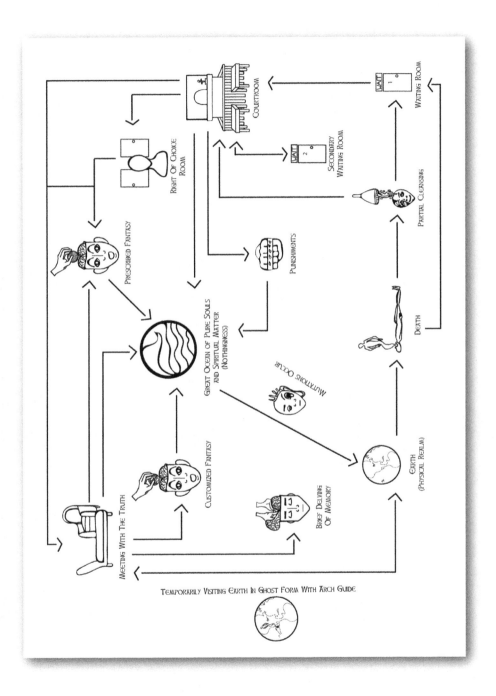

Part VI

One

The judge scratched his head in what seemed to be a struggle to arrive at the decision of whether Walter Klein would retain his Right of Choice. This decision was actually easy. The judge had made up his mind before Walter stepped in front of the podium. Instead the judge was puzzled by the same question as the other spiritual beings: Why was there a Special Focus placed on Walter Klein? What was it about him that was special? Was it something he had done or something he might do before the end of his processing?

The judge was hoping he would come to a realization in a timely manner. There were varying degrees of Special Focus on souls and The Truth often rewarded those who could discern the reason for it. People like Martin Tomlinson would have a large Special Focus put on them to the point where the reasons were obvious. Any guide or judge who knew even a little bit about the soul in question could usually infer the reason for such a focus. Thus, The Truth would not offer a reward for such cases.

In cases like Martin's, The Truth used a brand so everyone was aware of the Special Focus rather than only informing the guides and judges. The brand wasn't necessarily a symbol of horrific deeds such as mass murder, though. Branded souls were often agents of significant change in the physical world, people who shaped society such as politicians, famous musicians and activists. Other times they merely committed sins of which were lost in gray, sins that would take more time and deliberation to decide if they would cost the soul his or her Right of Choice.

As for the rewards of discerning a Special Focus, they varied immensely depending on what the spiritual being desired and how difficult it was to infer the reasons for the Special Focus. Some guides who were dissatisfied with their duties or tired of them received their wish of being done with their service, of being able to pass on into the great ocean or receive a prescribed fantasy the way normal human souls did. The Truth also promoted guides to judges as a reward for their insight, especially if it was a guide like Francis who enjoyed his duties and had ambitions of gaining more power and influence in the spiritual world. The Truth gave smaller rewards for less difficult tests. These rewards could be anything from allowing guides more time to observe souls or giving them more breaks between guiding souls.

Spiritual beings notified The Truth of their discoveries the way they attempted most other communications. They closed their eyes and focused on sending a sort of mental message directly to The Truth. They let their minds go blank until all they could hear was the sound of their own mental voice speaking clearly. The Truth would then receive the message and speak to them if they were to receive a reward. It was like a prayer that actually worked.

Walter's judge was almost ready to give up on sending such a prayer.

"There really is *nothing* special about him," thought the judge.

"Wait! 'Nothing'! That's it. The answer was so simple I overlooked it."

The judge's eyebrows rose and his ears twitched, forming the classic Eureka expression. He considered sharing his revelation with Vincent but was unsure about whether he wanted to give up the possibility of a reward. The Truth would most likely catch him anyway and realize Vincent wasn't the one who realized why Walter was a Special Focus soul. Now that he knew the answer, there was no point in delaying the trial.

"Walter, do you have anything to say before I tell you your fate?"

"No, your honor. I'll take what's coming to me."

Two

"Very well then. Walter, your transgressions are minor compared to other souls I've dealt with. Your sins did not do significant damage and you spent plenty of time atoning and repenting for them on Earth. Your mother's boyfriend recovered from his injuries, so there was no permanent damage. I also took into account the good deeds you performed in caring for your wife and the attempted reconciliations with your mother. You will retain your Right of Choice. Vincent, please take him to post-judgment."

"Thank you. Thank you!" said Walter.

Vincent began walking silently toward the door and Walter followed him. He didn't say a word about the trial. Walter looked over his shoulder and saw another pair of guide and soul rising from the bleachers and approaching the podium. It was lackluster.

"You're quieter than usual," said Walter as they neared the door. "You're not going to congratulate me?"

"The result of the trial doesn't surprise me. I knew you would most likely retain your Right of Choice."

"Why didn't you say so earlier? I was sweating a little back there."

"I thought you would be able to predict the result after gaining experience watching the other trials. I suppose I shouldn't expect anything of you. I'm also much more interested in why the Special Focus was put on you. Do you have any thoughts on that? I might as well ask you now that your journey is ending."

"I have no idea. I don't even completely understand how that whole thing works. It seems like it's more for famous people."

Vincent grunted in response to Walter and then reached for the brass knob on the door to post-judgment. The same indescribable vortex Walter had seen other souls enter now waited for him. Vincent ushered him through the door, stepped in behind and then closed the door. Walter gasped as he took in the surroundings and became a bit nauseous. He looked back at the door, which appeared suspended in air for a moment. It now stood on its own, without a wall, in a room that stretched on infinitely in all directions except downward. The guides and other spiritual beings referred to it as a "room" or "The Choice Room" despite it not having a defined ceiling. The floor was clear glass but it showed no reflection and it was too thick to be transparent. It almost looked like a hybrid of ice and glass.

Vincent put his hand on Walter's shoulder to calm him.

"It's a lot for a human soul to take in at first, isn't it? You'll adjust quickly, though. This is one of the areas of the spiritual realm where the façade of humanity begins to fade away because the coding is not as thorough. As I explained before, everything you've seen thus far is only a representation of your experience on Earth designed to make souls comfortable until the end of their journey. What you are seeing now is slightly closer to the reality of the spiritual realm. It is part of what purely spiritual beings such as myself can perceive at will, in addition to the simulations you experience as a soul."

"It's really trippy," commented Walter.

"Trippy?"

Walter laughed hearing the proper Vincent say such a word.

"Like 'strange.' Like tripping on LSD."

"You've have not used any illegal drugs, Walter. Remember, I know everything about you. There's no point in lying." Walter rolled his eyes.

"Geez, there's no limit to your stinginess and nitpicking. I'm just saying people are supposed to see weird things like this when they do drugs like acid. My friends described it to me. I wasn't trying to lie."

"I see. I'll explain the rest of this room then." Vincent had already become bored with the tangent he indulged and was eager to continue the process.

Vincent gestured to Walter's left before continuing. There were three identical doors, the same as the one Walter entered from. The one closest to Walter differentiated itself with a silver knob. The one in the middle had no knob. Its hinges could not be seen. The rightmost door had an obsidian knob.

"The door with the silver knob is for me," began Vincent. "It will transport me back to the part of the spiritual realm where guides reside and are assigned their souls. You won't be able to enter that door. The door without a knob will open if The Truth wishes to meet with you, me or both of us. In this case, it will open after you make your choice but before you enter the last door. You do not need to meet with The Truth if this happens. You may decline the meeting and proceed directly to the final door. The last and final door is the one with the obsidian knob. This will take you to nothingness or your prescribed fantasy depending on your choice. Only you should be able to enter this door."

"Seems pretty straightforward," muttered Walter. "What about the one we came in from?" he continued.

Walter turned around and was startled to see the door had vanished.

"There is no need for that door anymore," replied Vincent. "The Truth adjusted the system so the door returning to the courtroom and other spiritual areas would become inaccessible after judgment. Powerful souls like Mr. Tomlinson have attempted to escape and roam the spiritual realm. Thus, such a measure became necessary."

"So this is really the end. I can't even hang around a bit."

"That's right. Speaking of 'the end,' it is time for you to make your choice. What will it be, Walter?"

Walter's mind inevitably conjured memories of his wife.

Walter saw a chestnut haired woman playing a guitar as he was walking home. She must have been his age, maybe a little older or younger. She was playing "Blackbird" and her case was full of money. Anyone with working eyes would describe her as at least somewhat attractive.

Walter stopped and stared at her. The oncoming foot traffic hit him and he stepped toward her, nearly joining her against the wall of the music store. He only had a five-dollar bill. He wanted to give her all of the five dollars but also needed a few dollars so he would have enough left to spend at the hotdog stand he'd been eyeing. He placed the five in her case and she smiled.

"Thank you," she whispered under her breath after singing "learn to fly."

Walter proceeded to sift through the money in her case and extract four single dollar bills as he placed the five. He wanted to contribute and still have enough money for a hot dog. She raised her eyebrows in amusement, but Walter thought she was upset. As she finished her song, Walter shuffled the money into his wallet. He had been curious as to how she would react. Still, he immediately regretted the indulgence and decided to apologize.

"I-I'm sorry. I just-I would give you five dollars, but then I wouldn't have money for lunch."

"Oh don't worry about it. You could've gone to the bank if you needed change for your five, though."

"I guess you're right. This seemed quicker, though, and then I get to give you money at the same time."

"Well I'm glad to help. Glad to be your bank."

"Thanks. Wait, are you being sarcastic?"

The chestnut haired woman giggled and covered her mouth with her right hand. The base of the guitar swung like a pendulum as she released it.

"No I'm not. I've just never seen anyone put money in and then take some out. It's funny."

"Oh. I can give you five if you want."

She laughed again. "Oh my God forget about the money. I'm not mad I swear."

Walter blushed. "OK, I will. I'm Walter by the way."

"Susan. You know if you really want to help me out, you can take a CD on your way to lunch."

Walter picked one from the basket next to the case. It had a black and white photo of her holding a sunflower that obscured her face.

"I want to be a music teacher, but I'm doing this to help myself through school."

"Where are you going?"

"UCSD."

"That's impressive. I wanted to go there."

"You're in school too?"

"Yeah. I go to State," said Walter with marked lack of enthusiasm.

"For music too?"

"No, for business management. But I play piano on the side."

"Cool. Maybe we can play together."

"I'd love that. You don't know how good I am yet, though. What if I suck?"

"That's OK. I've got a good feeling about you. Here, let me give you my number."

"Umm…you sure you wanna do that?"

"What do you mean?"

"Er nothing I'm just not used to attractive women giving me their number."

"Well I can not give it to you if that's what you want," she began coyly. "And thank you, Walter."

"No, no, I want it," said Walter as he scrambled through his backpack to find a pen and paper. Susan giggled again.

The scene felt surreal to him. There was something about this woman that moved him in an unfamiliar way. Maybe it was subjective. Maybe there wasn't actually anything so extraordinary about her. Still, for the first time in his life Walter believed he was experiencing something that surpassed the limits of his imagination.

———

Walter was ready to make his choice.

Three

Walter lowered his head and studied the ethereal surface below him. The texture looked soft and inviting, yet Walter had a feeling the material was impenetrable. He could stomp and pound against it for a millennia and it would appear untouched.

"You know, Vincent, I was never good at much. I stunk at sports when I was a kid. I struck out when I played baseball or tripped over the ball when I played soccer. I wasn't good at tests. Even with piano I felt I reached my limits pretty quickly. I worked hard at everything I did, including my job, but I didn't have any natural ability or talent for it, or much passion. I even failed as a son."

He raised his head and smiled, looking into the infinite plane that stretched before him. It had no limitations, no walls or obstacles to overcome. People could wander in it for eternity. The problem was its emptiness and the fact he couldn't stay in it forever.

"Then I met Susan. I was good at making her laugh and smile. I was good at listening and responding. I was good at making her happy and making sure she understood how wonderful and beautiful she was. I was good at doing things she wanted me to do. I was a great boyfriend and an even better husband. That was who I was. That was all I was. That was all that mattered to me... and when she died, I had nothing. I *was* nothing... and I guess that's what I've wanted to be since she passed away."

Walter looked at Vincent before continuing. Then he glanced at the doors.

"It's not like I didn't consider the prescribed fantasy. It was tempting because I thought it might be a chance for me to live a second life, one where I wasn't a failure. I imagined having a fulfilling career, being successful. Then I thought about the nature of success, what it means to be successful. And you know what? I was successful. I was a great husband."

Walter thought of his conversation with David, a man who failed to be faithful to his wife.

"There are some people who don't have any success, any positive aspect of their lives to define them. Susan gave me everything I needed. I don't need anything more. Nothingness is perfect for me."

For the first time, Walter saw Vincent lose a bit of his composure. His eyes darted around. He crossed his arms and began tapping his right hand on his left elbow while he paced around. His expression became wild, frustrated.

"Damn," hissed Vincent. "That was why he was a Special Focus. I'm such a fool. I should've seen it. Maybe then I could get a meeting. I don't want to be manipulated like that, though. Damn!"

Vincent didn't care if talking to himself made Walter uncomfortable. He continued pacing, hoping it would help him more quickly work through his thoughts and emotions, as if his thoughts were tangible objects that moved with his body.

Opportunities for securing a meeting with The Truth were rare. During the course of his relatively long career as a guide, he'd only had a handful of opportunities and had missed them due to his stubbornness. The encounter with Walter once again made him reconsider his attitude. Participating in The Truth's system of rewards for spiritual beings turned his stomach but was worth it if it meant securing a meeting and perhaps an end to his service as a guide.

As Vincent finished processing the lesson he had learned from his journey with Walter, his pacing slowed. He took a slow, deliberate breath and regained his composure before returning his attention to Walter.

"So you are choosing to end your existence entirely? You're choosing nothing?" asked Vincent.

"Yes."

"I am surprised you have not chosen to live in a fantasy prescribed by The Truth. All of the souls I have guided thus far have chosen that option. I am having trouble understanding why it is not tempting for you. Wouldn't you desire to experience a life with the possibility of seeing your wife again? Wouldn't you at least desire a life without cancer? Isn't taking the chance better than nothing?"

Walter was tempted to throw Vincent's line about "asking too many questions" back at him for a moment. Vincent was upset, though. Walter decided it was best to answer immediately.

"Well, I think deep down I was glad I got cancer. After my wife died, I didn't feel like I had a reason to live anymore. I thought about killing myself and joining her in the grave. I mean, I really thought about it. I thought maybe I would get lots of attention by jumping off a big building and making a big deal out of it. You know, might as well make it count because you only get to kill yourself once. I even thought about doing it the same way I saw in the movies, you know, where the guy sits in his car, turns the engine on, and floods it with gas or something like that. I didn't have the guts, though. Having cancer made me feel better about that somehow. I figured that the disease would make the decision for me and I wouldn't have to worry about the shock and sadness people would feel if I killed myself. Even though my Mom had disowned me, I knew it would hurt her that much more to find out I had killed myself. As for the fantasy life without cancer, wouldn't I know it wasn't real? I think that would defeat the purpose. Also, you said The Truth prescribes it, right? That means there's no guarantee my wife would be there because I'm not designing the fantasy. What if I'm not worthy of having my wife in the fantasy?"

"Most of what you've said is correct. There is no guarantee your wife would be in the prescribed fantasy. Souls are also aware of their memories in the physical realm and carry these memories into their experience in the prescribed fantasy. In other words, you would have memories of your wife even if you were prescribed a fantasy without her. I'm surprised and impressed by your insight, Walter. I didn't think someone like you was you was capable of such induction."

"What do you think I was doing while we were sitting through all those trials? I was mostly thinking about the choice in case I got to keep it."

"I see. So you would rather accept nothingness than choosing an option that did not have a certainty of seeing your wife." Vincent phrased this as a statement rather than a question now that he understood Walter's resolve.

"Yes. Besides, I had my time with her already. I want more, but only if it's exactly like it was while I was alive."

"You're a strange man, Walter Klein. You don't make any sense to me. I would not make your choice in such a situation. Nonetheless, you've earned my respect. Your resolve is impressive. It is souls such as yourself who make me abhor this system, humans and my duties a little less."

"Thanks. I know how much it means to get a compliment from you. I'm sorry by the way."

"For what?" Vincent was puzzled.

"It seems like you wanted me to make a different choice. You looked upset when I told you I wanted nothingness."

Vincent was embarrassed. He regretted his display of emotion.

"Let's not talk about that more than we need to," said Vincent. "I was upset because your choice should have been obvious to me. If I had predicted it ahead of time, something beneficial might have happened to me. That's all."

"I see," said Walter. "I wish I could've made the choice that benefited you."

Walter laughed. He shook his head a little.

"What's so amusing?" asked Vincent.

"I really was destined to fail at every part of my existence except my relationship with Susan. I couldn't even do this afterlife thing right."

"That's enough, Walter!" snapped Vincent. His reaction surprised Walter. Vincent took a deep breath.

"I apologize for losing my temper. You see, I have guided many humans over the years, too many to count. Most of them see their spiritual processing as some sort of journey. They romanticize it. They treat their mundane human existence as if it were some sort of story millions of people would love to read. It nauseates me. When they begin perceiving it as a journey, they assume they need to change before they reach the end, or maybe as the journey is ending. They assume a journey only has one benefit: the opportunity to change. They think maybe their meaningless lives will have more value if they take this opportunity."

The discussion piqued Walter's curiosity.

"What are the other benefits?" asked Walter.

"There is at least one other benefit I can think of: an opportunity to maintain convictions, to see them in a different light and reappraise them, perhaps with value that was not apparent before. If a conviction is not foolish, I think there is value in maintaining it. I apologize if my earlier reaction made it seem like I was criticizing your decision. I do not think your feelings for your wife nor your decision are foolish. I actually understand them better than you might think. That is why I am your guide."

Walter processed the information for a few moments before continuing to indulge his curiosity.

"What was her name?" asked Walter. His tone was playful and friendly.

Vincent laughed heartily. This surprised Walter, who was still used to seeing Vincent cold and reserved. He wondered why his guide found the question so hilarious.

"This is goodbye, Walter. Go ahead and walk to that door."

Vincent motioned toward it.

"Turn the obsidian knob and enter," he continued.

"I guess I shouldn't push my luck," said Walter. "Goodbye, Vincent. It's been interesting."

Walter extended his hand. Vincent took it and they shook firmly.

"I hope you find what you're looking for," shouted Walter as he walked away and neared the door with the obsidian knob.

As he approached, the door without a knob, the one leading directly to The Truth, swung open violently. Walter was stunned for a moment. He then looked at Vincent, expecting him to give advice. Vincent was similarly stunned into silence so, Walter decided to address him.

"What should I do? Should you come with me?" said Walter, less loudly now that Vincent was walking toward him, intrigued by the occurrence. Walter felt a bit awkward now that their goodbye had become false.

"Perhaps," responded Vincent. "I haven't seen this happen in a very long time. I haven't met with The Truth since I became a guide." There was excitement in his voice. His pace quickened as he neared the door. The same indiscernible mixture of light and color seemed to await him. The moment Vincent stepped within a meter of the door, however, it slammed shut as violently as it had opened, smacking the threshold and somehow not making a sound nor producing a gush a wind.

Vincent's fists tensed. He ground his teeth. His eyes became even wilder than before. Veins began pulsating around his head and neck, forming a crude frame for his face.

"Damn you! Damn you, you arrogant prick!" screamed Vincent. "Are you scared? Are you scared of answering me?"

As Vincent stomped around, he moved away from the door. The moment he moved out of the radius, it opened again, but only for Walter. It was as if The Truth was taunting him, extending a rope into his pit of despair and then yanking it back as he reached for it. This further angered the already frothing Vincent.

"Fuck you, you cowardly bastard! I will find a way out! I'll be free! I'll beat you! Just wait!"

Walter was stunned, flabbergasted after witnessing Vincent's outpouring of anger and emotion. It was an anger exploding without control.

Walter approached Vincent, intending to comfort him with a hand on the shoulder.

"Don't come near me!" yelled Vincent. "Don't touch me! I'm not allowed to harm humans, but I swear I will use every ounce of my strength to break that rule if you get any closer!"

Walter became terrified.

Vincent saw this and attempted to calm down long enough to send Walter to his fate.

"I'm sorry, Walter. Please go on. I need a few moments alone. I'm sorry our goodbye had to turn so sour."

Walter backed away slowly, keeping his eyes on Vincent. Vincent couldn't stand Walter looking at him anymore. He walked further into the expanse of the "room" until he was a multi-colored dot in Walter's vision. He planned to return to the door with the silver knob once Walter had left. For the first time since his journey through the spiritual processing system began, Walter pitied Vincent. He began to understand his bitterness.

He turned around to see the door to The Truth was still open, beckoning. He realized he didn't need to have the meeting. If he wished, he could proceed to what he believed was nothingness.

Walter neared the door and stretched his hand through the void before entering. The void bathed his fingers in a strange texture. It reminded him of the sensation and memories of snow falling on his bare hands before it hit the ground and became part of the mixture of sludge and salt nesting outside the little mountain town shops in Julian, a town close to San Diego. It invited him in through the rest of the door. He was breathless for a moment. The void swallowed him. Then, a new room materialized and he inhaled the novel air.

Four

Walter recognized the room as his therapist's office. He had gone a few times before he met Susan and after his mother kicked him out of the house. It looked exactly the way he remembered down to every minute detail: the cheesy local art sculptures of seals and other marine-related San Diego landmarks, the wall filled with diplomas and certifications, the comfortable leather couch and parallel office chair. It was exactly what one would expect from a therapist's office.

Therapy had helped Walter control his curiosity and impulses so incidents like the one with his mother's boyfriend would not happen again. Nonetheless, the therapy had not erased the thoughts or extinguished the desires. Only death and the power of spiritual cleansing were capable of that. Walter reflected upon this as he scanned the office.

Walter jumped as the office chair whirled rapidly around to reveal a man who looked like his old therapist, Dr. Goldberg.

"Sorry, Walter. I can't resist surprising souls with the classic Bond-villain chair spin. It really never gets old," began the man who looked like Dr. Goldberg.

"So…are you The Truth?" Walter replied nervously.

"Indeed, I am."

"Then why do you look like my crotchety old therapist?"

"I chose this form because I thought it would make you comfortable and, admittedly, so I could play that little joke on you. I'll be serious from now on, though."

"What's your real form look like?"

"I couldn't describe it to you nor could you perceive it as a human soul."

"I guess that makes sense. Thanks for taking the time to chat with me by the way. I'm sure you're a busy guy."

"There's no need to thank me. At this moment, I am occupied with around one-trillion tasks. What you're seeing now is only a fragment of my being. I don't mean to belittle our meeting. I only want you to understand that meeting with you is not an inconvenience for me."

Walter scratched his head and averted The Truth's glance for a bit, not knowing what to do or what to say. It dawned on him that he was standing before a superior being. The conversation would not be between two humans despite the form The Truth had assumed. Yet The Truth's avatar felt like a normal human soul. It did not have the intimidating aura of the serial killer in the courtroom or the alien feeling of Vincent's spiritual body. Nothing about it appeared artificial because the craftsmanship was so perfect. It was the embodiment of Walter's memory now animated and possessed by a sliver of this being, the arbiter of an entire dimension.

"Please, sit down," said The Truth, gesturing toward the couch. Walter took a seat and began to relax. "Feel free to take the time to ask a few questions if you like. After that, I'll tell you why I brought you here."

"What's going to happen to Vincent?" blurted out Walter.

"You know, he was once much like you, Walter," replied The Truth with a grin. It was not trying to change the subject but rather seizing the opportunity to discuss something more interesting.

"Really?" Walter's face lit up and he laughed at the irony.

"Indeed. It's one of the reasons why I placed him with you. Vincent was much more successful, but he also became consumed by love to the point where he defined much of his role in life through his lover. Unfortunately, his lover was taken away and lynched."

Walter's stomach lurched as he imagined how he would feel in Vincent's place. Walter's wife had died in a car accident. It wasn't even a drunk driver. The road was slippery after some unexpected rain. Her car lost control and flailed around like a fish on a dock until it tumbled into the ocean. Walter would've wasted his time being angry at the rain or loathing the road for its ignorance. Even during the most violent throes of grief when rationality tried to leave him, he knew her death was no one's fault.

Like The Truth, Walter believed luck was the cruelest and most powerful force in the world. Yet luck was faceless, emotionless, void of intent and thus incapable of persecution. It had not discriminated against his wife and killed her out of bigotry and fear. The wet asphalt had not hunted her down, bound her like an animal and then raised her up like a scarecrow in a field. The cliff hadn't watched as men and women stripped her clothes off, continuing through her crying and screaming. The sedan hadn't whipped her and prodded her nor had it set her ablaze until she stopped moving, burnt to a lifeless pile of meat. Walter had not watched from the cliff, unable to reach her. Although her death pained him immensely, his wife's dying moments were not a horrible memory branded into his soul for decades nor were they an amalgam of humanity's cruelty and ignorance.

"After his death, Vincent always hoped they would reunite in the afterlife, even if it were only an illusion created in a prescribed fantasy," continued The Truth. "He suspected I paired you with him for that reason. That is why he did not consider your choice of nothingness. He believed you would make the same choice he would, given the opportunity. He thought you would take the chance to see Susan the same way he would take the chance to see Jeremy."

"Jeremy? Wait, Vincent is gay?"

"Yes. Like most gay men, he was born into the wrong era, resulting in his partner's persecution and ultimately his own death."

"How did Vincent die? That was what I meant to ask before I distracted myself."

"He took his own life. Perhaps it was because of the grief of losing his partner or perhaps he knew his community would execute him soon as well. Maybe he wanted to die on his own terms."

Walter imagined the pain he would've felt had his wife been taken in such a way and because of her sexual orientation. Perhaps then he would've had the nerve to kill himself. He, too, might have attempted to deny his ties to a species capable of such atrocities.

"That's horrible," replied Walter. "I guess that must be part of the reason he hates humans so much."

"Indeed. He hasn't accepted these memories completely, though. He believes I fabricated them."

"So what's going to happen to him?" asked Walter after a short pause.

"Souls earn their Right of Choice, so must guides earn their freedom from service if they wish it. Vincent has to prove he can overcome his bitterness before I can release him from service and grant him a prescribed fantasy. All guides earn their Right of Choice and can choose between nothingness and prescribed fantasy the way souls can. The difference is spiritual beings have the added choice of continuing their duties or seeking a promotion."

"You can't do anything to help him? I'm sure you could."

"Listen, Walter. I've learned from centuries of experimentation that there is no perfect system. Even the best systems create the disenfranchised. There will always be some who are bitter and choose to question and rebel. There will always be those like Vincent. It seems unfair for me to change the system that most spiritual beings are happy with only to appease him. Besides, you should have faith in him. Overcoming such bitterness and prejudice is a great challenge given his memories of Earth. Nonetheless, I am confident he will triumph someday. He was an incredible thinker during his life in the physical realm."

"You've got a point. I guess all I can do is wish him the best."

"We should shift subjects, Walter. After all, I did not give you the option to speak with me primarily so we could discuss Vincent. I guided you here because I enjoy chatting with Special Focus souls. They tend to be interesting. Most importantly, I did it because I wanted to offer you a little treat before your non-existence. You've chosen nothingness, but I am willing to allow you to experience one small memory with your wife before you pass on. The memory will be exactly how it was. It won't be a prescribed fantasy."

Walter lit up and nearly shook with excitement.

"Really?"

"Yes, really. I suppose receiving such kindness from me might be hard to believe after what Vincent has said."

"Yeah, he didn't have the nicest things to say about you."

The Truth smiled. "Despite what some human souls and spiritual beings believe about me, my main mission is to make worthy souls happy. I want to give them what they desired but did not receive in the physical realm. Now then, tell me the memory you want."

"You don't know already? I thought you guys could watch everything we did."

"I can't read minds, Walter."

"You can't? If that's the case, how'd you know I'd pick nothingness?"

"It was an educated guess based on observation. I saw you staring at the ground many times when you were on high buildings, considering suicide no doubt. Desire for death in the physical realm is similar to desire for nothingness as a soul. This is part of the reason I was so disappointed in Vincent. He had the same unlimited ability to observe you. He should've been able to come to the same conclusion as I did. He clearly was not diligent enough in his duties as a guide."

"Now then, let's get on with this. Time may flow differently in this realm, but is does still exist. I'm afraid I can't speak with you much longer. Please tell me which memory you'd like so I can finish processing you."

Although The Truth could have put aside more time for Walter, it had decided not to. It only did so for souls who had questions about the world, about all of the events The Truth had observed throughout history. Most souls did not take the opportunity to touch upon this. The processing primed them to be introspective. In their final moments, what mattered was confined to their experience.

"He's the one who wasted time with pranks and now he's rushing me," thought Walter. He decided to take advantage of the fact that The Truth couldn't read his mind. "Which memory should I pick though? There are so many moments with Sue and me." The answer struck him as he recalled the sensation of walking through the door to meet The Truth and the vaguely icy texture of the Choice Room.

"Could I relive the time me and Sue went to the mountains on that day trip? You know what I'm talking about, right?" said Walter.

The Truth reclined in its chair and closed his eyes. The lids twitched rapidly. It was searching through the near limitless data it had access to, refining the search and then narrowing down the list of memories until it had only one. After a few seconds, it opened its eyes.

"The trip you made to Julian. That's a good choice. Walk out the door you came in from and you'll be there. I've already arranged it. You'll experience the memory and then fade into nothingness."

"Do I get to spend the whole day?"

"You'll have a few hours. You'll be able to tell when your time is nearing an end."

"OK then. I guess I'll get going."

Walter wondered if he should say anything more before leaving. He didn't have time to develop any sort of bond the way he did with Vincent. There was only one thing he needed to say.

"Thank you. Thank you so much. You know me, so you know my wife meant everything to me. Thank you."

"You're welcome, Walter. Now go. Enjoy it."

Walter smiled. He about-faced and once again walked into the shimmering, breathless, void.

Five

Walter's surroundings gradually became visible. The almost blinding light he saw during his entrance to the void was now dying down. It was as if someone had flashed an old camera in his face. His hands were on a steering wheel. He was wearing a coat. Snow was collecting in thin sheets on the hood of his car. He knew exactly where he was. He was exactly where he wanted to be.

Among the many qualities Walter loved about San Diego and its surrounding towns, he loved that it existed on the midpoint of a spectrum with big cities on one end and small, quiet towns on the other. Susan used to call the idea of these amalgams on the ends of the spectrum, "Cityslickersville vs. Bumblefuck County." Walter always got a chuckle out of that.

San Diego was cultured like LA but without the smog, paparazzi and unbearable traffic. The downtown area had a bit of the grandeur of New York, but the people were nicer, not so much in a rush and the weather was unrivaled. People complained if the temperature rose above eighty or dropped below forty-five. It did not snow in San Diego, but it didn't matter. If people wanted to experience true winter weather, all they had to do was take a day trip to a nearby mountain town named Julian, maybe stay a night at a bed and breakfast if a day wasn't enough.

Julian had a single main street lined with all its most popular restaurants. The street was the thick stem that ran through the town with all the residential areas and smaller businesses protruding from it. It was all delicious comfort food, unhealthy but too pleasurable to stay away from. There was a Gold Rush-themed diner with big burgers, a pie factory, a sweets emporium with more than twenty different brands of root beer and horse drawn carriages that trotted slowly through the main street.

Walter could smell the food on him. He could taste the residue of apple pie, hot chocolate, cider donuts and his favorite: chocolate brownies with cinnamon ice cream on top. He realized it was the point in the day where he and Susan had finished gorging themselves in the town and then decided to use the additional drive further into the mountains as an opportunity to digest so they wouldn't be running around in the snow immediately after eating. Walter marveled at The Truth's power. After all, none of this was real. The true event had happened already. It felt real, though, indistinguishable from the actual event. The only difference was he retained his memories and knew what would happen next.

Walter wasn't startled when he heard a light rapping on the passenger seat window. It was Susan. He reflexively brought the window down so she could speak.

"Hey babe, do you have a little extra cash in your wallet? The parking here is more expensive than I thought."

The current of the memory was gently guiding him. He reached into his wallet and knew three dollars would remain. He knew it would be exactly what she needed. He handed it to her and she smiled. He photographed her face as she left with the money. Her chestnut hair, the little freckles on her cheeks, her tanned skin, her lucid green eyes — it was all the same.

Tears flowed freely from his eyes and his chest began twisting and knotting. Walter decided not to fight it. He worried about Susan seeing him and being concerned or confused. Then he remembered how long it would take her to return and knew he could let himself be moved. Walter wailed and sputtered. He coughed and moaned until he could taste the salty tears that had split off from the river flowing along both his cheeks. He reached for tissues in the glove compartment, knowing they would be there.

By the time Susan returned, Walter had dried his tears. She opened her door and slid the parking receipt into the dashboard. Then she looked at Walter, grinned and said, "You ready for me to kick your ass in a snow ball fight?"

Walter grinned right back. "Two points for the chest and three points for the head. One point for crotch and leg shots. Five points for the back and game over if we get a butt shot. Thirty-minute timer. Sound good?"

"That's a little different then last time's rules, but I'm game."

"Great! Let's go."

One of the many qualities Walter loved about Susan was her playfulness. They were together for years before she died, yet Walter could not remember a time that was boring or a time where they lost their spark. They always found something to do. Walter grabbed her hand, pulled her close and kissed her roughly before she put her gloves on. He wanted to take the opportunity to feel her touch before they started snowball fighting. She wasn't expecting the kiss but happily accepted it by putting her arm around his waist.

After half an hour of snowball fighting, they were tired. The timer on Susan's phone went off, but they didn't remember who scored more points. Both collapsed in the snow together and held hands. Walter's eyes widened as he saw bits of the mountain evaporating in a sort of fog. His car began to fade away along with the parking deposit station. He craned his neck around to see the top of the mountain was drifting into nothingness as well. He remembered The Truth saying he would know when the memory was coming to an end and realized this was surely it. He turned to Susan, almost in a panic, and decided to make sure there was nothing left unsaid.

"Sue, I'm about to leave. Supposedly I'm going to be nothing. I've accepted that. I'm a little skeptical, though. The whole system was so weird and I'm not sure what to trust. I was never sure what was completely real and what might be possible afterward. I'm rambling, though. Let me get to the point." Walter took a deep breath and rolled over a little so they were facing each other.

"If you're out there still, if some version of your soul somewhere can hear me and if I don't become nothing, I want you to come and find me because I swear I would spend the rest of my existence looking for your soul if I could. I love you. I love you so much. Maybe I didn't say it enough because I didn't think you would be gone so suddenly. I thought I would have decades to say it. I love you, Sue. I love you!"

Walter's surroundings began to fade into a color he had no name for. The nothingness was closing in on him. Only the patch of snow he lay on remained. He looked beside him to see Susan was gone. Everything around had broken into fragments of the nameless color. He attempted to sit up only to see his legs had vanished. He was not frightened, though. They had dissolved without pain. It was relieving, like he was about to drift into the most peaceful and dreamless sleep of his life.

He closed his eyes and felt the rest of his body cease to exist. And then he felt nothing. And then he was nothing. He was as nothing as he could be.

Author Biography

J oseph Rauch studied creative writing at New York University. His work has been featured in *Mr. Beller's Neighborhood*, *The Huffington Post*, *Vice*, *Psychology Today*, and other publications. He lives in New York City.